She
Dims
The
Stars

amber l. johnson

D1113411

Dedication

To the ones who see the light in the darkness.

No matter how small the beam may be.

I'm restless. Things are calling me away.

My hair is being pulled by the stars again.

– Anais Nin

Prologue

Elliot

I hate that skirt.

I've hated that skirt since the first day we met. She was wearing it and I swear that's what I was staring at and not her face. But she caught me looking, and instead of telling her how ugly it was, I ended up getting her a drink and then partially carrying her back to my dorm where she proceeded to pass out. I, being the gentleman that I am, took off the ugly plaid thing and put her to bed. I left her a note, reassuring her that I hadn't touched her, and she was more than welcome to the Gatorade my roommate and I had in the fridge.

Then I fell asleep in my ratty desk chair, and I guess, maybe, I figured I'd wake up to her screaming about being in a strange bed only half dressed. But instead, I was startled awake by her poking me in the forehead. She'd stolen a pair of my pants and was holding that pleated atrocity in her hand while she handed over her number and asked me to call her sometime.

And now that she's broken up with me, she's dancing in the middle of a circle of guys. In that ugly-ass skirt.

It's an affront to the year we were together.

It's the final middle finger; the last fuck you to our dead relationship.

I wish I had burned it.

"Excuse me."

I'm too caught up in my hatred of yellow and orange plaid that I don't hear the voice in time to sidestep whoever it is that's trying to squeeze between me and the sticky tiki bar I'm leaning against. When I turn too quickly, all I see is a flash of pink hair and two arms flying toward my face. I'm quick, though, and before this pushy person can make it all the way to the floor, I've got her by the waist and am hauling her up, smashed against my chest, face to face with *her* face full of hair.

The strands begin to fall away and dark eyes emerge, squinted and leering as she wheezes out a barely audible, "Thanks."

"No problem." I start to let the stranger go, but she presses in closer, her mouth angled toward my left ear.

"I can't feel my lips. Can you?"

I pull back a bit, my attention on her mouth as she presses her lips together and then apart a couple of times, like she's testing her theory.

"I'm not wasted, so I can feel my lips just fine."

She grins, and suddenly her hands are on either side of my face, and her eyes are in direct alignment with my own. "I didn't ask that. I asked if *you* could feel *my* lips." Before I can even come back with an answer, she's kissing me as hard as she can, gripping the back of my neck. Her tongue tastes like fruit, and she scrapes her teeth along my bottom lip when she lets go. Pushing up on her toes, she speaks into my ear again. "Let's run away."

I'm so caught off guard that the words are stuck in my throat, and I gently push her back to appraise just how drunk this girl is. But the way her eyebrow is raised and her lips are pursed leads me to believe she's not half as bad off as she was pretending to be. Her nose wrinkles a little as she tilts her head and sighs.

"You just cost me five bucks."

"What?"

"Five bucks if you kiss me. Ten, if you say you'll leave with me. Now how am I going to buy the next round?" She shrugs and pats my cheek before dipping below my elbow and disappearing into the crowd.

I stare for way too long, trying to pinpoint where she's going to emerge in the sea of bodies. But she never does. And for one fleeting moment, I forget that I've just been dumped.

Elliot

This blows.

My plans for the summer had not included sitting in my roommate's car for a four-hour drive so we could stay at his mom's house for a couple days. He planned to do his laundry and grab some old furniture she's offered to give us for our apartment. Our couch has a distinct odor, and she won't visit because of it. I don't mind the smell at all. Probably for that very reason.

This is a much shittier plan than going to Ireland with my girlfriend for four weeks.

Ex-girlfriend, I mean.

"Don't help or anything. You should just keep sitting there crying and staring out the window like a little bitch. It's really helpful." Cline grunts while he pulls his full clothes hamper across the carpet and gives up on it halfway to the door.

"I'm not hauling your dirty boxers up two flights of stairs. We might be friends, but I don't even like you that much." It's a lie, but it gets him to stop glaring at me. He's right, though. I've been staring out the window at the house across the street for about twenty minutes while he got the rest of his stuff out of the car. I'm not devastated or anything. Pissed about plans falling through? Yes.

He stands in the middle of the room and scratches his neck, probably because he's trying to grow a beard, but it's patchy, like, even his body thinks it's a bad idea. I have no clue how he lived in this tiny bedroom for so long before college. He isn't a small guy, and his head almost touches the globe on the out-of-date ceiling fan. It's as if his body takes up two-thirds of the available space.

"Mom's not getting back until later tonight from her shift. What do you want to do?"

I'm staring back out the window, watching as a black Honda pulls into the driveway across the street. Cline crosses the room in two seconds flat and yanks the dusty blinds down.

"Seriously, Elliot. Can you get it together long enough to survive this weekend? She was awful. I always hated her. She laughed like a donkey, and her Keds smelled up your room all the time. Also? I saw her bra on the floor once, and she wasn't even *trying*, if you know what I'm saying."

It was true. I hated her plain beige bra. And her laugh. I liked other things, though.

"It's not even about *her*. It's about Ireland."

He raises a hand toward the window and shoots me a look. "You see that? That's called sunshine.

It's mandatory for good health or something. Being in a place where it rains all the time with a girl who smells like Fritos is not my idea of a fantastic summer. Suck it up." He leans against the wall and mutters under his breath before speaking louder. "I'm getting beer. You're going to stop bringing me down even if I have to get you black-out drunk to do it."

"It doesn't rain all the time there." I mumble in response. I flop back onto his bed and pull a pillow over my face until the smell hits me, and I throw it across the room while trying not to gag. Beer would be good. Beer and video games and maybe a little hacking into Chelsea's Facebook page to tag her in some really unflattering pictures from her sorority parties she was always so quick to delete herself from. She really is only photogenic from the left, anyway.

I must have fallen asleep, because the sound of something at the window makes me shoot straight up in a panic. I listen, the quiet of the house causing my heartbeat to sound a thousand times louder in my ears. Thinking it is a fluke, I go to lie back down when I hear the noise again. There is a ping against the pane, and I slip off the mattress and slide over to the curtains on my knees, pulling two of the blinds open with my fingers. I can't see anyone from my position, but when the next rock connects with the glass, it hits right in front of my face. I jump a little, and my fingers get stuck in the slats, causing them to pull away from the wall and come crashing down on my knees while I try to scramble away.

Silence fills my ears, and I stand, embarrassed and disoriented until another rock makes contact. There is *no way* the person below didn't hear or see that. The window pane is stuck, and I have to push as hard as I can before it gives way and I am looking down at the lawn where a girl is staring back at me, her right hand filled with pebbles.

"You're not Cline." Her head tilts to the side, and she squints up at me. "Did he move?"

"No."

"Huh. Are you … a friend?"

The way she says it makes me tip my head to mirror hers. "Yeah. Wait, *what kind of friend*? I'm his roommate."

Her eyebrows lift. "So you live together."

"I'm sorry. Was there a *reason* you were throwing rocks at the window?"

She nods, the mass of hair sitting on top of her head bouncing in the process. "I was going to ask if Cline wanted to come out to a party at the lake house tonight. But if you have other plans ..." She starts to back away and drops the rocks to the ground at her feet.

"I don't have any plans." I lean farther out the window and brace my arms on the sill. "My ex-girlfriend is going to Ireland without me over break, so I am completely plan-less." I really suck at coming across as cool or collected.

She stands in place for a second and then shrugs. "Then ask Cline if he wants to come. We'll be there at seven."

"Okay. But who are you?"

The way she smiles makes her look like she has a secret. "I'm Audrey."

She is halfway to the driveway across the street when I yell after her. "I'm Elliot, by the way!"

The only response she gives is a hand raised in my direction.

"No." Cline places the bag on the counter and shakes his head. "No. Just no."

"What else do we have to do?"

"There's plenty of stuff to do. We can play video games. Or … eat. Or play video games *and* eat. We can do anything other than go hang out at the lake with Audrey Byrd."

"What if you meet a chick?"

"No." He pulls the beer from the bag and sticks two in the freezer.

"What if I meet one?"

He pauses, fingers wrapped around the door

handle. "Maybe. It could certainly help your perpetual state of puss-itis."

I ignore his attempt at getting under my skin and counter with, "What if you get laid?"

He hangs his head and presses his face to the door while it closes. "Fine."

The bottles go back into the bag, and the two of us get into the car. One short stop at a store to buy some more beer, and we are on the road for the hour-long ride to the lake.

"How do you know her?" I turn to face his profile in the dark cab of the truck. The obvious answer is that they were neighbors, but he's acting like there is more to the story.

I swear I see his jaw tighten before he answers. "That's the thing. I don't know her anymore."

"Okay, but you did, right? Did you used to be friends?"

His eyes narrow, and he shifts in the seat, never looking away from the road. "Audrey Byrd and I were best friends from the time we were four years old until we were fifteen. And then one day she morphed into a psycho bitch who thought she was better than everyone and starting treating people like shit." He nods once. "That includes me. So, were we friends? Yes. Are we friends now? No. And I have no idea why she even came over to ask us to come to this thing anyway."

The whole Audrey thing seems like a pretty sore subject, so I drop it. He is quiet the rest way there, and I don't bother him. When the lake comes into view, I reach over and turn the radio down. "There are a *ton* of people here." I'm in awe. I was expecting something small. Maybe ten people at the most.

"Yep. Apparently she has a bunch of friends now." Sarcasm is dripping from his tone.

At least forty are outside of the house, drinking, talking by the bonfire or out on the dock, their bodies rising and falling with the sway of the water. I see Audrey standing with a handful of people, her head tilted back in laughter while she cradles a wine bottle to her chest. There is a moment where her eyes are closed, and I pause to study the way her face softens before her lids open again and her attention lands on us.

Cline makes a sound that is a mix between a sigh and groan, pivoting toward the house with the beer under his arm. I wait, watching Audrey cross the back lawn to make her way toward the house, where she comes to rest, a foot away from me. The wine bottle is a third of the way gone, and her cheeks are bright pink, leading me to believe she's had all of it by herself.

"You made it."

I shrug, tipping my chin at the house. "It was a hard sell, but I talked him into it."

Her eyes trail to where the door is open and she sighs, curling the bottle into her chest.

In a move to avoid the house—or Cline, I'm not sure—we start walking in the direction of the fire, and my palms begin to sweat where they've been shoved into the front of my hoodie. She hands me a beer from the cooler, and the cold can takes away all the heat. "Does he hate you or something?" I take a small sip and wait for her to answer.

She grins and then arranges her features into a serious frown. "He's probably still mad about that time I took his virginity when we were twelve."

The drink catches in my throat, and I turn my head to spit it out on the ground instead of at her face. I can't stop coughing, and she just stands there, smiling at me, while I struggle to breathe.

"I'm just kidding. He's probably still a virgin."

I shake my hand to get the beer off of it and clear my throat. "I can attest to the fact that he most definitely is *not* a virgin."

Her jaw goes slack, and her dark eyes go wide. "You've seen it."

"The sock fell off the door. It's really not my fault."

Audrey keeps eye contact as she tips the bottle back to take another swig.

"He's surprisingly limber for a guy his size."

That time, she chokes on *her* drink. "Oh, no. This story is horrifying. Given the type of girls at Brixton, I can only imagine who he brought back with him."

"You know about Brixton?"

Her eyebrows draw together and she laughs. "Yeah. I go there, too."

"I've never seen you." The beer is going down easier than before and, without having to ask, she hands me another one.

Her fingers feel warm against mine when they brush. She stares right into my eyes when she responds. "It's a big campus."

Even though there are a ton of people around us, it feels like we're the only two at the party. That close, next to the bonfire, I can see every one of her features. She has long black lashes and these freckles across her nose that make her look really young. Her face is round, and she is shorter than I thought she'd be up close. But her hair catches my attention the most. The ends are light blonde, and the top is dark brown. I can't figure out if she's too lazy to take care of it or if she's paid someone to make it look that way.

"You should go mingle." She begins walking backward in the direction of the dock and raises her depleted wine bottle like she is toasting me. "You're a free agent, Elliot! Lots of ladies here to rebound with."

She's right. I'm a single man, and there's a ton of alcohol within reach. There are plenty of girls here. And once I have beer, my confidence grows and, suddenly, every girl around me looks a hundred times hotter than she did when I first stepped out of the car

The rest of the night kind of goes by in a blur, but one thing I'm sure of is that I'm spitting mad game at a redhead on the couch who is three co-conut vodka cola's deep. Her eyelids are heavy, and she pouts almost constantly, opening one eye while we talk, like she's trying to make sure I'm only one person because she thinks I may be a twin.

She seems interested, but then she gets up to go to the bathroom, and I don't see her again for the rest of the night.

Cline, though. Cline is a massive guy and wouldn't be what girls consider conventionally attractive. But his personality makes up for it. At some point, I see him with a girl on the other side of the room, and I try to maneuver my way over without tripping on any furniture. I make it to him just in time to see him lean into the girls face and tug on the end of her white-blonde hair before he asks, "Nice shoes. Wanna fuck?"

The funniest part about this line is that the girl isn't even wearing shoes. But she laughs so hard that she falls into him and, within minutes, they're walking down the hallway to find an empty room.

I'm not suave by any means. Chelsea was kind of a one-off, if I'm being completely honest. I never in a million years would have pictured myself with a girlfriend as hot as she was.

I'm too goofy. Too awkward around girls. I

don't know. I've been told I'm many things. A good flirt is not one of them.

I can't recall what I said to the girl with the black hair by the bonfire, but it ends with us running to the lake to drunkenly jump off the dock and me being pulled out of the water by someone who looks a little like Cline. Maybe it was my old stand-by of "I like that shirt, but I'd like it better on my floor."

Pretty sure that's when I blacked out. Which is a shame, because the girl who wanted to go swimming had actually taken off her top.

Elliot

"Elliot."

I shift and press my face into the fabric under my cheek.

"Elliot. Elllll-iiiii-ottttttt." Whoever is making an E.T. voice is going to get my full wrath. As soon as the room stops spinning, of course.

This time it's a whisper right next to my ear. "Elliottttt."

It startles me, and I jump a little, my eyes flying open at the sound of little pings as something scatters across the floor.

Audrey. Audrey is by my side, laughing hysterically as I sit fully upright and watch a hundred Reese's Pieces rain down around my feet.

"Original. Where the hell did you even get this many Reese's?"

She blinks and leans back, her mouth open in false shock. "What else do you eat while you're drunk?"

The house is eerily quiet, and I squint under the terrible brightness of that asshole we refer to as the sun.

She gets to her feet and tilts her head to look me over. "You're really bad at this drinking thing."

"I don't do it very often, but when I do, I commit." The smile I give her is fleeting before the back of my throat tingles, and I'm stumbling up and towards the bathroom to prove her right.

She's standing outside the door when I finish

puking, and the amusement on her face can't be ignored. "Cline left you. Said I could bring you back to his house."

"Why?" I'm only vaguely aware that my legs are really cold.

"He said something about wanting to choke you out, but then you passed out on the couch, and he went back into a room with that girl again. He took her home this morning. Said there wasn't enough room in the truck."

"He really is the shittiest best friend on the planet."

She grins. "The. Absolute. Worst. I made him a t-shirt that said that exact thing once."

"You're the one who bought him that? He wears it all the time." Just chuckling makes my head hurt, and she pushes off the wall tsk-ing as she walks away. "Why am I only wearing boxers? Where are my clothes?" I'd be embarrassed if I wasn't feeling like death.

"Someone brought them in from outside. You

weren't wearing much when you were dragged in here."

When she returns, she has a cup full of stuff that fizzes like Alka-Seltzer but tastes like really bad Gatorade. I assume I'll puke this up in about five minutes, but miraculously, after laying down for another fifteen, I am perfectly fine and asking about breakfast.

In the time it's taken me to recover, she's cleaned up what she didn't get to before waking me. If I wasn't in so much pain, I would be really impressed with how pristine the place looks before we shuffle outside. When she locks the door behind us, I can see this look cross her face as though she's disappointed that we're leaving already. Her eyes fixate for a second on the welcome mat, and then, like a light switch, she turns to look at me with a smile.

"You're a dude, so I assume breakfast means bacon. With a side of bacon. Am I right?"

I'm surrounded by fast food biscuit wrappers, and the taste of grease sits heavy on my tongue while I let the wind hit my face at sixty miles an hour. Audrey has graciously not spoken until this point. And then …

"What was her name?"

I crack an eye open and roll my head in her direction, hoping that the look I am giving her is one of disdain and not one where I look like a lobotomy patient. "Who?"

"The girl." Her eyes slide to me and back to the road. "The one you were screaming out the window about. The one who made you try and pick up every last girl at my party last night." She smiles a little. "Unsuccessfully. But still."

I groan and lean my head back against the car seat. "Chelsea."

"I'm sorry. Kelsey?"

"Chelsea," I say louder. The sound of my own voice makes my head throb, like the hangover is just waiting to come back with a vengeance, and my body is ninja-ready.

"We'll call her Kelsey. I hated a girl with that name once."

My eyes are filmy when I blink them open to look at the delight on her face.

"Like a code name. That Kelsey Bitch. Ugh. She's such a *Kelsey*."

"You're crazy." I laugh and close my eyes again.

She responds almost too softly for me to hear, "Yeah. Maybe." Then she elbows me. Hard. The car veers a little into the other lane, and I grab the *oh shit* handle and press my foot to the dash.

"You're a terrible driver."

"You're a bad pick-up artist."

"What?" I straighten up and face her profile. "I have amazing pick-up lines."

She makes a face. "Is that why so many girls

were into you last night? Because all I heard was a bunch of stuff about boobs and dragons."

"'Do you like dragons' is one of the greatest pick-up lines on the planet."

"You're delusional. There are a million better ones than that." She rolls her eyes and turns on her blinker to take the exit off the freeway.

"Sure, there are. Like last week when some chick said she couldn't feel her lips, and then asked me if I could. Then she kissed me."

The car jerks as her foot hits the brake and she turns to stare at me as she slows to a stop at a red light. "No way."

"Awful, right? So the dragon line is a thousand times better than that."

Audrey's cheeks light up pale pink and she averts her eyes. "Oh, yes. Telling a girl you'll be dragon your balls across her face later is probably the better of the two. But I suggest maybe you work on your game a little bit harder if you want to get over Kelsey."

Cline is acting as if I killed his childhood pet and mailed him the head. He's barely spoken a word to me since Audrey dropped me off at the house. Just grunts and an occasional sarcastic remark every time I try to engage him in conversation.

The ride back to campus should be fun.

We have everything packed and ready to go when he finally addresses me. "Let's get outta here." He shoves his ugly-ass fedora on his head and swings the front door open as though it has offended his mom and he's exacting his revenge.

I figure it best not to bring up Audrey anymore until I can figure out just exactly what the hell his problem is. But I don't have to mention her at all.

She's standing outside, leaning against her car with a huge pair of sunglasses on her face. In her left hand is a purple Popsicle, and she has it pressed between her lips as she watches us load the car.

"Hey, Cline!"

He turns and regards her with a scowl on his face. "What?"

"I like your hat!"

He angles his neck like he's not quite sure if she's offering him a compliment, but he raises his hand and runs his fingers along the brim of the thing on his head. "Really?" It's sad that he seems a little hopeful that she means it.

She laughs and shakes her head. "No. It's awful. You look like an idiot."

He opens his eyes wide, and his mouth follows as he pretends to reach into his shirt pocket. His hand emerges, and he's holding up his middle finger, looking surprised by what he's found. " *You're* an idiot," he mumbles and turns back around.

I can hear her chuckle clear across the street. She motions for me to cross over to her, so I do, my hands shoved into my pockets, because she makes me a little nervous.

Audrey tips the melting dessert in my direction.

"Tell him the fedora isn't working. Save him some embarrassment. "

"I've tried."

"It's a shame. All that male ego … You, on the other hand." She rolls her head to the side, and I wish I could see her eyes as she looks me up and down. "I like those glasses on you."

"My contacts are ruined. I don't wear these glasses much." The weight of them on the bridge of my nose causes my nostrils to flare.

"You should. But lake water will do that to contacts. I should have warned you. I mean, I would have if I had known you were going to get trashed and try to swim at two o'clock in the morning. But I'm not a fortune teller or anything."

I kinda think ruining my contacts was worth her compliment, but I don't tell her that.

She holds out the Popsicle in offering. "Want a bite?" If she's asking, then I'm not going to say no, so I dip my head and bite into it, pulling away to smile, grape sugar coating my tongue.

I press my thumb to the side of my mouth and clean off the bit that has escaped. Her eyes are staring as I do, and I'm quiet for a second, lost in thought before she laughs and finishes the rest of the Popsicle off.

"What are you thinking about?"

I grin, and I'm brave looking at her. "I'm thinking that right now, at this very moment, I know what your mouth tastes like."

If electricity could crackle between two people, there might have been a sound. But all I hear is the hush of her soft exhale followed by a sticky-lipped whistle. "Best one, yet, Elliot. You should invent something to carry around with you so you can have these on hand at all times just so you can use that line. Like some kind of insulated fanny pack for frozen treats." She waves the stained stick in front of my face.

The moment loses its magic, and I find myself laughing at the idea of her invention. "Yeah, maybe. That would definitely get my mind off *Kelsey*." I say it just to see her smile. She doesn't disappoint.

"See ya around, Elliot." Audrey's cheeks push her sunglasses up higher on her face when she grins, and then she turns around to go back inside her house.

The taste of grape lingers in my mouth for the entire ride back to college.

Audrey

"So, you're good?"

My weekly call with Cara usually includes this phrase, and it's been a while since I've answered it honestly. She knows when I'm lying anyway, but when I tell her that I actually am fine today, I can hear the hint of surprise in her otherwise flat tone. I'm itching to get off the phone by the time she asks the next question. There's music pouring from an open door as I pass by, and I know she can tell I'm not at home.

"Where are you going?"

"Crazy. Wanna come?"

She doesn't laugh at the joke. I don't expect her to. She just continues with her rundown.

"How are your impulses?"

I cringe and rest the phone between my cheek and shoulder so I can wipe my palms on my back pockets. "Great. Everything is great. Actually, I have to go, so … talk next Tuesday?" She agrees and hangs up, but I'm left feeling anxious as I stare at the brick building in front of me and try to get the nerve to dial another number. It only rings once before he answers.

"Audrey?"

"Hey. Yeah. I mean, yeah, it's Audrey. Hey. What are you doing?"

There's some movement behind the curtain as I'm looking up at it, and I can see his shadow rise from what I assume is a chair by the window.

"Getting some stuff together for a project. What

are you doing?"

I take a deep breath and expel it with a laugh. "I think I'm standing outside your place. Wave at the window." The shadow moves closer to the curtain, and I can see five fingers spread as he waves. "Yup. That's definitely you. Unless this call is being tapped, then that's not cool at all, and this is how a horror movie would start."

Elliot moves the material aside and opens the window, peering out at me from above. "Do you always communicate through windows?"

The smile on my face could shatter my lips. "Not always. Just on special occasions. Let's run away. Come on."

He leans on his elbows and cradles his face in his hands, his adorable brown eyes looking me over. "I have a project."

"You're no fun, Elliot Clark."

Lips pursed and eyes narrowed, he nods. "Where were you thinking?"

I shrug and hold my arms out like we have the

entire world at our fingertips. "Honestly, I just want some pancakes. And that's maybe a five-minute walk. I'd settle for that."

Not once has he asked how I knew where he lived. Or how I found out what his last name is. I don't know if that should put me at ease or make me more nervous, so I try to shut the thoughts down altogether. Which is hard, because sometimes I think all I'm made up of is a constant train of thoughts.

We don't talk much on the way, and that suits me just fine. He's a watcher, and I stare at his profile as he takes in the other students walking by us or hanging around in groups. They're drinking or smoking or talking too loudly. His face is an open book, and it's like I can see inside his head exactly what he's thinking about all of them as we pass by. His eyes roam some of them from top to bottom, and I wonder if he's putting their physical attributes somewhere in a file in his brain for later use.

When we reach the diner, he seems to snap out

of his little people watching trance and finally acknowledges that I'm by his side. Elliot's smile is endearing and a little shy as he holds the door open for me, his height so much greater than mine that I don't even have to duck beneath his arm to enter. Not that this is much of a feat. At five foot three, I can walk under most guys' arms. I'd bet Elliot stands just under six foot, though. Still much shorter than his roommate.

His fingers fidget as he scans the crowd before resting his hand gently on my lower back and leading us to a booth in the middle of the restaurant. The table is sticky with syrup and the air is thick with the smell of bacon and eggs. His lips press into a thin line while he pretends to read the menu, but his eyes are wandering elsewhere, and I sit back to watch him some more. He's wearing contacts again, his dark brown eyes peering across the top of the menu and looking beyond my shoulder.

"Do you have a huge bacon boner right now, or is there someone behind me that you're freaked out about? I can't tell if you're scared or horny."

His eyes flick to mine and a look of terror crosses his face. "I assure you, the two are not mutually exclusive. Sometimes they go hand in hand, but right now, my ex is sitting two tables to the left, facing me." He raises the menu a little higher and tries to shift down in his seat.

"Huh." I try to play it cool, but I fail at that kind of stuff, so I just end up turning around and looking for whoever this girl must be. There are three of them, and two are exceptionally pretty. One is average. I assume with the way he's about to lose his shit, he dated one of the hot ones. I turn back around, and his face is completely obscured by the menu now. "Blonde or super blonde?"

"What?" His eyes reappear and he blinks a bunch of times.

"Is it the hot blonde one or the hot super blonde one? Because I'm assuming that the third wheel is only there to make the other two feel secure about themselves, right? And that can't possibly be your

Kelsey-Chelsea."

His entire face is visible now, and his mouth is hanging halfway open. "Are you a witch?"

I laugh and shake my head before leaning back against the seat. "So which one?"

"Super blonde," he says quietly and averts his eyes like he's suddenly really intent on figuring out what kind of topping he wants on his pancakes.

It makes sense, though. Elliot would be totally pressed about being dumped by a girl of that caliber. It has to be a blow to the ego. And he's such a nice guy. I don't even know the girl and I already hate her.

Truth be told, I don't really know Elliot all that well, either.

I scoot out of my seat and into his, pressing myself against him, hip to hip. He's stone still, staring straight ahead like he's afraid if he moves I'll attack him. His eyes slide in my direction, his long eyelashes raising higher as they widen, and I hear him faintly whisper, "What are you doing?"

I clear my throat and turn a little before resting my hand on his. "Let me just say one thing before we do this, okay?" He nods just the slightest bit before I continue. "I am in no way attracted to you. And this doesn't mean anything. Now say something funny."

He turns to face me so fast that our noses almost brush. "Funny."

"Good enough." I squeeze his hand and let out the loudest laugh I can possibly muster. I flip my hair and laugh harder, gripping his arm even tighter and angling against him until I'm almost in his lap. *Good lord, his biceps are much larger than I remembered from the lake house. Or maybe I just wasn't paying attention. I need to focus.* "Oh my God, Elliot. You have got to be the funniest guy I have ever met." I drop my voice and stare at his lips which have gone dry. They're not bad lips. Fuller on the bottom but wide … *Focus, Audrey.* "Funny guys are so hot," I say as loud as I can. And then I'm on him. Straddling him in that nasty diner seat, my ass squeezed against the table as I press my entire body against his and hover my lips over his.

He's freaking out, and I can tell his fight or flight reflexes are starting to kick in, so I press down on his lap even harder to ground him there. And then I kiss him. My heart is racing, fluttering upward and getting lodged somewhere in my throat. I know I've kissed him before, but there were drinks involved. And money. This is just kindness, or something, on my part, but he's not giving me anything to work with, and it's making it a thousand times harder to pull this off.

I pull away and lean into his ear, nip his lobe, and whisper, "Kiss me back, or she won't buy it."

"Ohhhh." It's an exhale and then his hands are on my back pressing me closer, his lips finding mine. I don't think he means to, but his hips raise a bit and I have to push back against him because I can feel the table lift up a little. It settles down with an audible screech, but he's not paying attention, because he's figured out that I'll let him put his tongue in my mouth and he's really, *really* into it.

I bite the tip of his tongue gently and he pulls back a bit to make eye contact. He's red-cheeked and breathing heavy, and my lips feel five times bigger than they did before. I stare at the beauty marks on the side of his face while I find my sense of gravity again. My hands are in his dark hair and I'm … yeah… I'm pretty sure his hands found their way up the back of my shirt. His hands are *big*. Shit.

"So … did you need more time to look over the menu? Or …"

I turn to look over my shoulder at the waitress who has her arms crossed and an eyebrow raised. It's not like she hasn't seen worse. But I have a brief thought that maybe we put on a pretty damn good show. And that means we got the job done. My pelvis rubs against Elliot's jeans, and I hear him make a strangled noise.

I pretend to be embarrassed "Sorry. I think maybe we'll just get ours to go." I climb off his lap and make eye contact with the super blonde who is definitely staring. Without a thought, I rattle off an order like I know what my man wants.

The waitress smiles and reaches for the menus, but Elliot hesitates. His menu is now in his lap, and he shakes his head quickly. "I'll keep this for a minute, if you don't mind. There's a puzzle on the back I wanted to look at."

We've been in his apartment for ten minutes, and he still hasn't spoken. He's eaten everything and refuses to look directly at me.

"I was trying to help you out, okay? I had no idea you'd get all weird about it." I have to break the silence or else I'll lose it. It should be noted that I also did not know he'd get a hard-on from the ordeal, either. I'd say that wasn't my fault, but let's be real.

"Are you really that upset that she broke up with you? Did you love her or something? Were you planning on popping the question?"

"No." He finally manages to look at me, though his gaze only lingers briefly. He clears his throat, and I see him clench his jaw once before he drops his fork and shoves his plate away with a sigh. "It's not like that. I'm mad that she broke up with me before we went to Ireland because it was supposed to be part of this project that I'm working on over the summer. It's why Cline and I kept the apartment instead of going back home. So, yeah, I wanted to go away for vacation, and I wanted to get the stuff for my project. I'm not hung up on her."

I point at the front of his pants and grin. "Well, that was obvious."

"Shut up!" It's the first bit of a smile I've seen from him since the diner. "You were, like, *on* it. You'd be offended if I didn't have a reaction. Be honest."

"I mean, I guess so?" This time we both laugh, and it feels like the tension is finally leaving the room. The weight on my chest is starting to dissolve a little. I always have such good intentions.

I take a moment to look around his place. The apartment is small. It's a two bedroom, and the living space is maybe a total of seven hundred square feet. I counted twelve steps to cross his threshold into the kitchen and another three to get to the couch. I haven't gotten a full view of his bedroom, but the door is cracked, and I can make out a couple of piles of clothes on the floor and a whole bunch of wires coming from everywhere.

My immediate instinct is to ask if I can help him clean his shit up but I tamp it down. Too soon.

Instead, I wander back into the kitchen and start opening cabinets. Three of them are stocked with nothing but cereal. A few different kinds, but there are at least three boxes of Lucky Charms staring me in the face, and it makes me grin.

"I'm the reason Cline got fat, you know," I say with a laugh.

Elliot turns and regards me warily, his gaze untrusting.

"It's true. His mom used to be this psycho, all-organic, holistic, no-sugar Nazi. So whenever he would come over to my house, I'd let him have whatever he wanted. You should have seen his face the first time he had an oatmeal cream pie. It was like he'd found religion. And then I gave him a soda … which didn't end well. I can't go into too many details, but apparently he went home and trashed his room. Wrote all over his walls. Jumped on his bed until it broke."

"What the actual hell?" Elliot appears to be genuinely concerned.

"I know! Caffeine, man. I told her he must have had an allergic reaction to one of her muffins." A laugh bubbles up in my throat at the memory of his mom dumping three trays of muffins in the trash while we watched from across the street. "She never made flax seed pomegranate gluten-free baked goods again."

He rises to his feet and leans over the back of the couch to look me over. Like, truly look me over.

The way he was doing with the people on the street. "You're a little crazy, you know that?"

My heart accelerates at his words, and I force a smile. "That's probably why I'm majoring in Psychology. I have a theory that people either go into Psychology to find out what's wrong with someone they love or with themselves. So ..." The confession causes my cheeks to burn, and I scramble to change the subject. "What's yours?"

"Game design. That's why I'm pissed Kelsey-Chelsea did what she did. I have this opportunity to present a game mock-up to this company after the summer. One of the characters was going to be based on her, and we were going to Ireland to get her family backstory to help flesh out her role."

I lean on the kitchen counter and purse my lips. "She's some side part you had written in as the love interest or something? Because God forbid you make her the main heroine in your game. Did she just not have a tragic enough back story?"

The moment the words leave my mouth,

Cline's bedroom door flings open and he steps into the room, staring at me but speaking to Elliot. I feel like it's the first time he's looked at me— *really* looked at me and seen me— in years. And my stomach instantly begins to tighten and sour.

"You need a tragic backstory, Elliot? Look no further. No one has a sadder story than this girl right here. Isn't that right, Byrdie?"

I'm glued to the spot, struck mute under his words.

Elliot moves closer, but I don't acknowledge him. "Dude. I thought you were out," he says.

Cline shakes his head and angles against the counter, facing me just a few inches away. "Forget your ex and her fake stories about having an uncle who was a count in a town that no one's actually heard of. *This* is your real story."

Elliot makes a move like he's going to say something, but I hold up a hand to stop him. I knew at some point I would have to talk to Cline about everything. I just didn't think it would be like this.

But if he needs an audience to make himself feel better, I can give him the satisfaction.

"He's right." I rip my gaze away from Cline's face and stare directly at the boy I've only recently come to know and like a little bit. Maybe I trust him. Maybe I've completely lost my mind. Either way …"You want a tragic story for your game? I'm totally your girl. Cline knows all about it. He was there for almost all of it."

It's the *almost* part that Cline never understood. It's the missing parts he's not aware of, because I've never been able to tell him. How do you explain to the person who has known you the longest that they know absolutely nothing about you at all? That he only knows what everyone else knows, and that it's absolute bullshit. Just surface.

I hold Elliot's gaze as I say what Cline wants to hear. What he's known his entire life to be true. I introduce myself as the girl he knew all those years ago. "My name is Audrey Byrd. Better known around my hometown as the Coma Baby of 1994.

The one who killed her mom at birth." I extend a shaking hand as my heart begins to hammer merci-lessly inside my chest. "It's nice to meet you."

Audrey

They say it takes a village to raise a child. In my case, it took the entire town of Bertram Falls to come to my father's, *excuse me*, Patrick's rescue and raise the little girl who was born to a dead mother and a grieving father who had no idea what he was doing. I assume, from what I've been told, he was barely keeping it together. As he did not have that motherly bond that most babies are afforded at birth, the transition at home was less than ideal.

The women of the town took over our home with almost round-the-clock care as my father grieved and tried to process his new role in life. The older I've gotten, the more I wonder why he didn't just give me up. I wouldn't have blamed him. Especially knowing what I do now. But perhaps when your front door is overrun with local news cameras and filled with the good intentions of local church women, cooking home baked meals, you can't reveal the truth.

You can't admit that you don't want this baby that has ruined your entire life.

He did a really good job of faking it. I'll give him that.

Whenever I think about my childhood, my home, I always remember it being busy and my house being full. There was never a quiet moment unless it was at night, and even then I was usually trying to sneak out of my window and across the lawn to get to Cline's and engage him in some kind of trouble.

We'd camp in the backyard or swim out at the lake house on the weekends when our parents would agree to it. He was my very best friend—my partner in crime—from the moment I could steal his toys in the sandbox. I knew everything about him, and the same could be said the other way around. We had no secrets.

There was even a time when we'd planned a sort of *Parent Trap* type of thing where we were going to try and get his mom and Patrick together so we could be brother and sister. But it didn't work.

I never used to believe in fairytales or evil stepmothers until Patrick met my step-Mom, Miranda. I would tell Cline how weird it was for me when they started dating. He knew exactly how uncomfortable it became in my house when Miranda moved in. Our little bubble, this world I had known where everyone in town was welcomed with open arms inside our home, suddenly became a place where no one was allowed to enter.

I was eleven when she first appeared, all tight

skirts and high buns that pulled her already small eyes even smaller. Her features, tiny as they were, were *severe,* and her eyes seemed to always be judging me. She never looked at me with anything other than disdain, as if I were a stain on her really expensive cardigan that she just couldn't get out.

Patrick's face, though long and thin, had once held an openness to it beneath his light blond hair and thin framed glasses. If eyes could be kind, his were. At least, for a while. It's truly amazing how stress can change the entire landscape of a face. How concern can bury itself into the corners of a person's mouth or eyes and etch its way into their skin until their soft lines become hard and they stop looking approachable.

Maybe I assumed that's where the changes started to come from in myself. Once they got married, it was hard to even get close to the man I once called my dad. Miranda and her couple's retreats. Miranda and her yoga for two. Dinners with clients and cruises that did not include me.

That's when everything started, I think. My therapist once asked me to pinpoint the first time I could remember doing something that I would consider "weird." I'd always had a thing for numbers. Counting steps. Counting the letters in words. I never even gave it a second thought.

When you're younger, you kind of think it's badass that you know exactly how many steps there are from your door to your best friend's lawn. Almost like you're a spy. Or some kind of math genius. At least it was like that for me. It was just who I was.

Who I am.

But after Patrick married Miranda, something shifted and everything became *so intense*. I think everyone blamed it on hormones. Like, how messed up is it that a girl gets her period and suddenly people are looking at her like it's perfectly okay for her to be exhibiting these behaviors that anyone else would be concerned about? But instead, Miranda was all, "Nah. She just needs some Midol."

Midol does not treat sadness of the magnitude that I began to experience. It does not take away the types of thoughts that began to surface in my mind as I was pushed farther and farther out of Patrick's orbit. I know what she told him. She would say that I was a teenager and that I was alienating myself, but it wasn't true.

I tried. I really did. I wondered if the things I was feeling were the same my mom had felt. And I wished that she had been there to talk to. I knew nothing about her. My grandmother had little to nothing to do with us. She made no small secret that she blamed me for her daughter's death. I blamed myself, too, eventually. Why wouldn't I? What else could have caused a perfectly healthy woman to just … coma out and die like that?

I was poison.

Miranda didn't even have to say anything after a while. I just knew. I was the reason for every bad thing in my family's life. Hell, for all I knew, I was the reason for every bad thing, ever. It wriggled its way into my brain, and I tried to fight it. The deepening darkness that started to surround me. Like I owed it to the entire town that had tried so hard to keep me alive for so many years.

Then it happened. I remember, clear as day, no matter how many times I've tried to push it away or how many times I've spoken with a specialist, the memory is so fresh it makes my chest physically ache.

Me, fifteen years old, sitting at the lunch table, holding a drink in my right hand and clenching my left. I don't exactly remember what I was looking at —probably nothing, because all I could think about was what Miranda had said about my hair before I had left the house. It was a dig, as usual. My self-esteem was in the shitter, and I'd started to count how long I could press my fingernails into my palm before it became unbearable, when I heard his voice through the haze surrounding my thoughts.

"Jesus, Byrdie. Do you not have a medium setting?"

Cline was leaning over the table, his ever fattening arms braced heavily on the wobbling fixture. I remember he was eating a candy bar and that his left front tooth was caked in chocolate.

The thick fog around my head seemed to settle over my eyes for a second, and I blinked it away, the soda can shaking a little as I turned to look straight at him. "What?"

He licked the food from his teeth and made a motion toward me, causing the rest of the people at our table to turn. "You're either up here"—he raised his hand above his head—"or down here." He pretended to bend down and place his palm on the floor. "Are you never just … normal? The fuck is wrong with you anymore?"

I don't know if it's because he finally noticed and called me out, or what it was, but having all those eyes on me as he said it sent a flood of panic, unlike anything I'd ever experienced in my life, rushing up through my sternum and into my esophagus. Tears sprang to my eyes, and my throat began to close. I swear, to this day, I could hear my heart beating inside my own ears, and instead of giving a sarcastic comeback, instead of telling him to go to hell and throwing food at him, I stood up really fast and ran out of the cafeteria, in tears.

The entire walk home, I practiced what I was going to say. I had questions and I needed my dad. I wanted to sit down face to face and ask him everything I'd ever wanted to know. I no longer cared if it hurt him to answer. Memories of my mom shouldn't have been things kept hidden and placed in dark boxes in my grandmother's house. I should have been able to know her. But I knew nothing. She was kind and sweet and had died too soon. These are the only things I had been told, and I mostly knew them because Cline's mom would tell me anytime I got the nerve to ask.

I'd had an entire conversation with my father in my head by the time I reached my front door, sweating and trembling with anticipation of what was to come. Patrick Byrd worked from home, but Miranda did not, so imagine my surprise when I heard them arguing in the living room as I walked into the foyer. I wanted to call out and let them know I was home. Wanted to announce my presence somehow. But the yelling rendered me mute.

"I can't have this conversation again, Miranda. You knew coming into this marriage that there would be no children."

Her voice was shrill and hateful in response. "No one in this town knows that you're sterile. We can use a surrogate."

"No."

There was a shuffling sound like something was being pushed. Maybe the couch. Maybe Patrick. I can't be sure, because my eyes were squeezed tight.

"You haven't had a problem raising another man's child for the last fifteen years. Why would it be an issue now?"

That darkness, that feeling of desperation I'd been fighting for so long, hit me in the chest like a physical blow, and it took every last ounce of strength in my body not to hit the floor in a crumpled heap.

I'm not proud of what happened after, but that was the day Byrdie ceased to exist.

Or, at least, it was the day I tried to make her disappear.

Elliot

It feels like all the air in the room has been sucked out with a vacuum. Cline is staring at Audrey with the most intense expression, and I'm trying to decipher if it's betrayal or disappointment. Like what she's just divulged came out of her so easily. She's just admitted to having one of the saddest origins I've ever heard of, and yet she's standing here, holding my hand and shaking it like we're making a business wager of some kind.

"Is that not tragic enough for you?" Her head leans a little to the left as she lets go of my palm. "There's more, if you need it. But I'd like to make a request for my character."

"Sure." It's really all I can offer at this point.

"I want my girl to ride a unicorn. And I want the unicorn to shit rainbow cookies as a defense."

The mental picture of Audrey atop a unicorn as it drops rainbow-colored cookie bombs breaks whatever heaviness there was in the room mere seconds ago, and I let out an awkward laugh that's a cross between a choke and a hyena bark.

"I'm serious. Cookie-shitting unicorn or nothing, Elliot." Her smile is shaky, but her voice is strong, and it does not go unnoticed by Cline.

"Are you being serious right now?" He is bracing himself against the counter, his full attention on the girl staring back at him with a blank expression.

"Yeah. If I'm gonna be in a video game, I want some artistic license. I have no idea what he was planning to do with the character of the ex, but I'm sure it wasn't half as bad ass as—"

"Shut up." He slams his fist down and steps toward her, making her take one back. "Just, *shut up*. Why are you even here? It's been, like, six years since you've even spoken to me after you ran away, or whatever, and now you're in my place and hanging out with my best friend. You're gonna ride a unicorn in his game?"

"If I can interject, there really isn't use for a unicorn in the game at all. It's a military game based off of my father's old journals." I raise my finger to stop them from going further, but it goes unnoticed.

"What part do *you* get to play? Are you the best friend in the game?" She's seriously asking, and Cline's face goes bright red. "You're a great best friend until you're not anymore."

"That's called projecting, isn't it? I took a psych class, too." He spits back at her.

The stand-off in my kitchen makes no sense to me at all right now. I notice Audrey's left hand twitch, and her fingers start tapping against her palm one after the other as she stares directly at Cline. It's a pattern, but I can't make it out. Suddenly, it stops and she turns to me.

"I don't have very much information on my mom. My grandma keeps all her stuff at her house in North Carolina, and she doesn't have anything to do with me since I'm the devil spawn that killed her only daughter. And if you want to know about my dad, I don't have any information on him either."

"Bullshit. What are you talking about? Your dad gave you everything you ever wanted. I know. I was there. You have been *so messed up* since you ran away when we were fifteen." Cline reaches out and pushes her shoulder just the slightest bit to make her acknowledge him again.

She braces herself before turning and facing him once more, some sort of helplessness in her eyes when she answers. "First, I'm glad the story about me running away has stuck after all these years. Patrick and Miranda did a great job selling that one. But since you're finally interested in the truth, my father didn't give me jack shit, Cline. Patrick Byrd took care of some other guy's baby because his wife gave birth to it. Put his name on it. I have no idea who my real father is.

"I don't know a thing about my mom. I have no idea who my dad is. And everything you thought you knew about me was a complete lie. How's that for some bullshit?" She addresses me again. "Sorry. Is that enough to get me onto a unicorn in your game or not?"

My room is a mess, and I'm trying to throw piles of clothes into the corner so Audrey can sit down at my desk. Her fingers are doing that thing again while she waits but I ignore it while I shove the last sock under the bed with my foot and turn around to face her. With both hands splayed open, I shrug. "Have a seat."

She's looking around the room at my sculptures and wirework, her gaze lingering on sketches of faces and some renderings I've printed off to work on during the break. "You don't suck at this, you know."

I scratch the back of my neck and sit heavily on my bed. It's been an insane night already, and it's not even midnight. Cline left the apartment, so it's just me and Audrey in my tiny-ass room filled with my stuff that only my roommate and my ex-girl-friend have seen up close. It feels weird. Like I'm naked, and not in the good way.

"I'm going to take that as a compliment, all things considered."

She smiles and continues to look around before reclining in the chair and folding her arms over her chest. "A military game, huh? Based off your dad's journals?"

"I didn't think you caught that with all the back and forth between you two," I admit.

"I caught it. Why are you doing it off his journals instead of asking him directly?"

My skin prickles, and I straighten my shoulders, because sometimes you have things in common with people in the strangest ways. "Because he died in combat and the journals and letters to my mom are all I have to go off of. He once wrote that he was right in the middle of Hell, and I just got this idea that I'd make a war game where the base camp was directly over the entrance to it."

"You believe in that stuff? Hell and heaven and whatever?"

I nod and look down at my hands before I speak. "Yeah, I do."

"That's just terrifying, don't you think? I mean … if there actually is a heaven and a hell, and the Bible says that after we die, we're supposed to keep existing forever, then … that's frightening. We are never going to stop existing. At the end of the day, at least I know I get to go to sleep. But the thought that I'm gonna have to be awake and keep doing this kind of stuff forever? I just …"

I look up in time to see her blink and wipe her cheek as she swivels away in the chair. The light from my computer makes the side of her face glow in the dim lighting of my room.

"Anyway. I'm sorry for your loss. That's what we're supposed to say, right? How old were you?"

"Eight."

"So you have some memories of him, then?"

"Yeah. Of course. They're few and brief, but they're enough to keep a picture of him in my mind. I guess that must be tough for you, right? You don't have any of your mom or … the guy."

She shrugs. "I have what I have."

"Have you ever talked to your dad about it? I mean, Patrick. Have you confronted him about the entire thing?"

Audrey shakes her head and focuses on the *Fallout* poster above my bed before she answers. "I've done enough damage. To be honest, I can't even talk to him about her. You can't say the name Wendy without him physically flinching. If I brought up the other-guy thing, who knows what would happen? We have nothing of my mom in our house. It's all at my grandmother's, and I'm not even allowed over there."

I lean back and cross my arms behind my head, looking up at the ceiling as I say the first thing that comes to my mind. "You should go anyway. I don't have anything to do over break. I can go with you."

I have no idea how my twin size bed withstands the weight as she jumps on me from across the room and makes me say five times in a row that I mean it.

Audrey

How exactly does one go about packing for a trip that could change the course of her life? I'm standing in my room, staring blankly at the empty bag on my bed, distracted by the blue constellation print of my comforter beneath it. I can close my eyes and know where every single thing in this place is. Yellow desk under the window; sheer curtains open and blinds pulled shut. Laptop, last semester's text books waiting to be sold, old papers and pencils all on the left-hand side. The right side remains clear. Silver desk chair pushed in until the metal touches the wood.

Nightstand to the right of the bed with one charger, a small lamp, and a place to take my jewelry off at night. One dresser behind me with a television. Small closet that holds just enough clothes to get me through the semester, because the other half of it is where I have shoved a bookcase full of fiction.

I open my eyes and idly wonder if I should bring something to read. It's a six hour drive to Elliot's house where we'll be getting his camping gear for the remainder of the trip. Another eight hours to Grandma Ruth's. The plan is wide open from there, and it makes my skin itch to not have some semblance of order to follow. I *need* order.

The thoughts of what could potentially go wrong start to gather in my head, and I can feel my jaw start to tense, so I close my eyes again and breathe in and out as deeply as I can in counts of seven.

It takes a few minutes, but I get a handle on it, and my heart rate slows enough for me to focus and silently begin to fill my bag with things I need to take with me. Not the least of which is a flower-printed bag full of orange bottles.

Elliot has an Xterra, and for some reason, that is unexpected. "You go off-roading a lot?" I ask, shifting my bag from one shoulder to the other as he checks the tire pressure on the front driver's side wheel.

He looks up and squints at me, one eye smaller than the other as his tongue peeks out between his lips. "No. Why?"

I resist the urge to roll my eyes. Instead, I push up on my toes and chance a peek inside to see if his car is as dirty as his room. It's not, and that, too, is surprising.

He stands and straightens his t-shirt, the material getting caught on his broad shoulders. "I cleaned it. Vacuumed and whatnot. Thought you wouldn't want to ride for that long with Taco Bell wrappers under your feet."

I pretend to swoon, pressing my hands to my chest. "And in that moment, I swear I fell in love with you, Elliot."

He tosses the pressure gauge in the air and catches it before giving me a dirty look. "A thank you would have worked just fine, smart ass."

"Thank you," I concede.

Suddenly, the door to their apartment is thrown wide open, and Cline, in all his disheveled glory, lumbers onto the sidewalk, half dressed and pissed off. Hazel eyes are barely visible as he stares us down, pointing a thick arm and long finger at Elliot. "Where the hell are you going?"

Elliot straightens his shoulders and faces his best friend, his neck tilted a little as they come toe to toe. Cline's extra two inches barely make a difference when Elliot mans up. Witnessing this makes something in my stomach flutter.

"I'm taking Audrey to North Carolina to her grandmother's house to see if she can get info on her mom."

Cline's eyes go wide, and his head snaps in my direction. "Granny Ruth? The psycho? She won't even let you near her house. How are you supposed to even—" He puts both hands up and gives a sarcastic frown. "You know what? I told myself that this was none of my business. I did. I said, 'Cline, man, this is none of your business.' But now you've roped my roommate into driving you, like, twenty hours to go see someone who won't even speak to you." He bounces a little on the word 'speak,' pulling his fists against his chest as his voice rises. "So *now* it's my business. She's using you, dude. Just like she does with everybody else."

"It's fourteen hours from Tennessee to North Carolina, actually," I correct him.

"And I volunteered." Elliot pushes the pressure

gauge into his pocket and crosses his arms like that should be it. Final. Over.

But I know better.

Cline bends forward at the waist, his arms crossed and knees bent again before he stands up straight and yells, "Oh! You *volunteered*. A fourteen hour drive. Okay. That's makes it okay. Got it. Well, wait right here while I go get my shit because I'm coming, too."

I think, deep down, *deep, deep* down somewhere in my subconscious, I knew this was going to happen. It is why I'm not even the slightest bit surprised by the outburst. I'm actually quite amused.

As calmly as I can, I move to the rear of the vehicle and open the back door so I can slide my bag inside. Peeking around the side of the car, I make a "shoo" motion with my hand.

"Hurry up, then. We haven't got all day. We're wasting daylight."

Cline's anger is apparent in the flare of his nostrils. "I'm seriously coming."

"I seriously don't care."

"I'm coming."

"You already said that." I walk around the car and over to where he's still standing in his pajama pants. "You remember when you were little and your mom wouldn't let you watch anything except movies from the eighties or before?" His eyes narrow and those nostrils flare again. "You're like that asshole kid in the backseat of *Adventures in Babysitting* right now."

"I watch whatever I want to now." He says it like he's so proud. It almost makes me laugh.

"Big man."

"I'm totally coming on this trip."

I sigh and wave a hand at the car. "That's fine, because I didn't have enough room in that bag for my Box Full of Fucks to Give. So would you go get packed so we can leave? You're starting to annoy me."

Elliot has been standing silently off to the side for the entire exchange, and finally he steps between us, placing a hand on my shoulder and one on Cline's chest. "I can't do this if you're going to act like a couple of eight year olds. Both of you need to shut up. And I mean that in the nicest way possible." He looks at me. "Please, get in the car." He looks at Cline. "You have five minutes to pack or we're leaving. I told my mom I'd be home for dinner." He steps away cautiously then pulls the car keys from his pocket. "If the two of you start fighting, I will pull over and leave one of you on the side of the road. Swear to God."

The car is dead silent for the first hour of the trip. Every time Elliot attempts to turn on any type of music, Cline vetoes it, so eventually he just gives up. The entire thing has started to give me a headache anyway, so I have taken to staring out the window and counting the numbers on license plates.

Everything must add up to seven. Any way that

I can force the numbers to sequence themselves, I do.

$$HBC6033$$
$$6 \text{ and } 3+3 = 6$$
$$6 \times 6 = 36$$
$$3 \times 6 = 18$$
$$8 - 1 = 7$$

An old rusted truck pulling a trailer eases alongside us before picking up enough speed where I can see the plate and start all over again. I don't even know how much time has passed as I continue to do this, but when Elliot reaches over and places his hand on mine, I realize that my fingers have been busy at work on my shorts. I've picked away a large chunk of frayed denim that now lies in a clump on his seat.

He pats my hand and keeps his eyes on the road as he hits the right blinker and pulls into a gas station. "I need to fill up."

As discreetly as possible, I scoop up the remnants of my destruction and palm them so I can throw it away as I walk by the trash can on my way inside the convenience store. Inside the bathroom, under the unflattering fluorescent lighting, and amidst the smell of years of uncleaned piss, I stare at my reflection. There's a huge possibility that I'm going to find out who I am. That I'll finally know whose brown eyes these are. Who this round nose came from. Whose lips in some lineage caused a cupid's bow to be so deep?

There's a possibility that I'll find out that the stuff inside my head isn't just mine alone.

I could find answers, and the thought scares me so much I have to brace myself on the sink for a moment before I remember how gross it is, and then I wash my hands a few times for good measure, just in case.

The cashier eyes me warily as I walk the aisles looking for snacks for the road. I wonder if Cline still eats King Size Snickers and chases it with a Dr.

Pepper like he used to back in school. As far as Elliot goes, I realize I don't know what kind of snacks he likes, but some Reese's Pieces might make him laugh. So I gather an armful of items and carry them to the register, a small smile on my lips as the cashier takes in all the sugar and beef sticks I've accrued.

"Road trip," I state.

His thick cheeks puff out as he rings up each item one by one. "Good choices."

Just the one affirmation that perhaps I've done something right makes me feel a little lighter as I walk back toward the pump.

"Are you in love with her or something? Because I've never seen you act like this before."

I know Elliot's trying to be quiet, but I'm close enough to hear him ask the question.

"No." Cline is adamant, and I go still, standing behind the partition, waiting to hear the rest of the conversation. "I don't love her. I don't even *like* her. As a person or as anything. That's what I'm trying to tell you. She will ruin your entire life, dude. One minute we were best friends, and the next minute I could have been a tree in her yard for all she cared. She acted like none of us existed anymore. Her friends. Even her family. She has a track record—that's what I'm trying to tell you."

Elliot puts the gas cap back on and closes the lid. I can see his hands from where I am hiding, and they disappear as he shoves them into his pockets and leans back against the car. I pull my body closer to the partition to listen.

"Let me just remind you that she threw a rock at *your* bedroom window that day, asking for you to come to her party, not me. I just happened to be there. She came looking for *you*. Maybe you'll get over yourself soon and find out why she was trying to find you instead of being such an asshole all the time."

I close my eyes and take a deep breath. Dr. Stark is staring at me from her chair, her pencil poised over her notebook as she waits for me to answer. She's asked what the next step toward forgiveness is.

"Asking," I reply.

Eyes open now, I make a big deal about shaking the bag and causing as much noise as I can, like I've just come around the corner. I dip my hand into the bag, and without even looking him in the eye, I press the candy bar and soda into Cline's chest and continue walking around the car to get back inside.

Elliot

The six-hour drive ends up being closer to seven, because Audrey's bladder is the size of a peanut. Maybe a cashew. Also, at some point, once we crossed the border into Alabama, I had to pull the car over and get out just to distance myself from their constant bickering. As I stood and watched traffic go by, I made the decision to render Cline's character mute in my game. Maybe sew his lips shut myself. Perhaps I'd just erase the mouth all together.

That thought is the only thing that gets me through the remainder of the drive to my house. We pull up in front of my little one-story home, and I take a second to look at it with fresh eyes. I try to see it like Audrey might. It's small, sure. But the lawn is well kept and my mother's flower garden is in full bloom. She keeps hanging plants along the front porch, and she's just had the front door repainted crimson red. It may not be the most glorious place, but it's ours.

The smell of chicken fried steak hits me as soon as I open the door, and I almost fall to my knees. I'm ravenous, and there is nothing better than my mom's cooking. Except maybe my grandma's, but she's been dead for a couple years now.

"Ma! We're here!" Without even thinking about it, I head down the hallway toward the kitchen, kiss two fingers and press them to my father's picture as I pass. "Are you in here?"

She's standing over a pot at the stove, her hair

pulled up into a clip, the steam from the pot making her curly hair even curlier around her ears. There's music on, and she's doing this thing with her feet that I'm sure at one time she thought was dancing but now it just looks like an unsure shuffle. I crouch down low and sneak up behind her, then grab her ankles and yell as loud as I can.

Her scream is even louder, and I swear she jumps a foot into the air, her arms flailing out, and the wooden spoon in her hand goes flying across the kitchen before it makes contact with the wall and bounces to the floor. Roseanne Clark, all five foot nothing of her, pins me with her icy blue eyes, her hands to her chest and breathing ragged.

"Hey, Ma." I go in for a hug but she slaps my chest instead. Then she pulls me in for a hug and pushes me away to slap me again.

"You're the worst," Audrey speaks up from behind me. She hooks a thumb toward Cline and shakes her head. "I should have made a t-shirt for you instead. You made your mom throw mashed potatoes at the wall, Elliot."

Mom thrusts a kitchen rag into my hand and then composes herself. "Clean that up. Set the table. I'm going to change my clothes, and then you can introduce me to your friends. Also, I agree. You *are* the worst." She hugs me again, turns around, and leaves the room.

Cline wanders over to the stove and starts touching pans. "I think you made her piss herself."

"Shut up." I start to laugh and then stop. *What if I did?*

"Earlier statement retracted. Cline still holds the title for The Worst." Audrey heads over to the cabinets.

I have just finished cleaning up the wall when I look over and see that Audrey has set the table for the four of us. She sees me looking and shrugs.

"I'm hungry and you're slow. I don't want to wait any longer because that smells amazing. I figured I'd help. No big deal." she says.

My mom reappears in different clothes, making

some excuse about not wanting to smell like oil or grease, but now I'm worried I *did* make her pee herself, and that only means that Cline is a shithead, because scaring each other is a thing with me and my mom. She woke me up for the first day of high school dressed like Freddy Krueger with one of the knife fingers pressed to my throat, telling me if I didn't get up she was going to turn me into a motorcycle.

Cline sucks.

Audrey and my mom have clicked and are talking up a storm while I stuff my face with as much good food as possible. Cline is watching the exchange with narrowed eyes, and I'm starting to get the feeling that maybe he's the problem in all of this. Not her.

My mom's a pretty open book. She'll talk to any and every one, and her body language is always welcoming. Audrey is responding to it, leaning in like she's stuck in her tractor beam. There's a fleeting thought in my head that it must be nice for her to talk to a motherly figure. No wonder she feels so comfortable.

"How is your game coming along?" My mom's attention is on me, and I chew what is in my mouth quickly to answer her.

"It's still in the early stages, but once I have everything I need, it should be pretty easy from there."

"That's why I'm here. Elliot needed another character for the game, so I said he could use me." Audrey smiles and it's genuine.

"What's it about again?" Mom asks before taking another bite of food.

Audrey opens her mouth to speak, but I cut her off to talk over her because I haven't told my mom anything about the real project. I have no idea how she'll respond to using my dad's old journals and letters. I don't know how it will affect her. So I say, "It's a fantasy game like Game of Thrones meets Candy Crush, and Audrey's character rides around on a unicorn and kills people with rainbow-colored unicorn poop cookies."

There's a barely muffled, "Jesus," from where Cline has his face buried in his hands.

My mom hardly bats an eyelash. "Turn it into an app, and I bet you'll make a million bucks."

Lying in my old bed feels familiar and odd at the same time. It's been this way every time I've come home for the last three years. Sometimes I wonder if my mom would like the extra space for a treadmill or an office, but then I'd have to sleep on the couch, and it would feel like this wasn't my home anymore, so I let her keep everything the way it is. Sometimes we need a little bit of constant in our ever-changing lives.

My bedroom door creaks open, and I turn over to see Audrey slip through the crack and close the door again as quietly as possible. "Sorry," she whispers. "Did I wake you?"

I sit up and reach for the light, but she waves her hand to stop me. "I wasn't asleep. You okay?"

She's hovering at the edge of my bed in these little shorts and a tank top, her hair pulled up into that mess on her head again. "Don't be weird, but can I get in with you? Is it against house rules to have a girl in your room?"

"Isn't your whole 'thing' —your whole existence—about breaking the rules?" I ask and pull back the covers to invite her in.

She slips between the sheets and rests her cheek on my pillow, so I turn and mirror her position, looking at her face in the muted moonlight of my pre-teen bedroom. This girl is really pretty, but she's full of so many secrets. Her eyes search mine for a moment before she inhales deeply.

"I'm working on that. I promise."

"Okay."

Her body heat quickly warms up the space between us, and the bed becomes toasty under the covers. I fold the comforter down a few inches, and she smiles up at me as she adjusts her hands under the pillow.

"How many girls have you let sleep in this bed with you?"

Eyes wide, I lean back and feign insult. "None. I would *never*."

"Liar."

"Fine," I concede in a whisper. "I've had exactly ninety-nine, so I was really hoping you'd come in here tonight so I could round out my number."

"You're an idiot," she manages out through her laughter. The bed shakes and creaks a little, so I press my hand on her hip to get her to stop shaking.

"Shh. The walls are thin, for real. I don't want my mom to think we're in here doing anything."

"Of course not." Audrey lies on her back and looks up at my ceiling for a few quiet moments. "I really like your mom. You take after her a lot. Mannerisms and stuff. She's nice."

"Thanks."

"Why did you lie about the game?"

I close my eyes and try to think of the best way to say it, but it's hard to explain without getting too detailed, so I decide to go with, "I don't know how she'll react to having a game made that's so close to real life for us. If you know what I mean."

"Sure. I get it. And I agree that the unicorn game would make a million dollars in the app store."

Now it's my turn to laugh, and she has to place her hand over my mouth to keep me quiet. She's hovering over me, our noses almost touching as she quietly speaks. "Thank you for doing this. For taking me to Ruth's. It means a lot to me."

I pull her fingers off my mouth and nod, curling her fist into mine and laying it on my chest. "You're doing me a favor, too."

"Is it safe to say we're friends, then? I have people I like or know, but I don't usually say I have many I would consider to be friends. But I think you and I are, yeah?"

Puckering my lips, I pull my eyebrows together. "I don't know, man. You stuck your tongue down my throat and everything."

"As a friend!" She whisper yells and pinches my side, making me gasp and jerk, then giggle before I man up and stop that shit.

"Alright! You stuck your tongue down my throat as a friend. Fine. Now, are you sleeping in my bed as a friend? Is this a friend snuggle here?" I motion between us.

"Yes. Now roll over that way so I can big spoon you. It's safer like this. Plus I can pretend I'm a jetpack while we sleep. Maybe you'll dream about being in outer space."

I do as she says, and she wraps her arms around my middle, but I pull her hands higher. "This is the safe zone," I tell her as seriously as possible. "I cannot be held responsible for the things my body does in the night or in the morning if your hands wander outside of the safe zone. Friends or not."

"Jesus take the wheel. This is going to be a long night," she pretends to cry into my back.

Then she starts making jet pack noises, and that combined with the warmth of her embrace helps lull me to sleep much faster than I care to admit.

Audrey

I had snuck back out of Elliot's room about an hour before we were supposed to be up and just rested on the couch with my eyes open, wondering what the day was going to bring. Three states are all that separates me from something life changing. I can feel it in the pit of my stomach as the rest of the people in the house begin to stir. A quick breakfast, a heartfelt goodbye, and we are on the road into the morning sunrise.

Saying goodbye to his mom was difficult for some reason. Her hug was warm and inviting, and maybe it was the way she embraced me and held me like she meant it, but I didn't want to let go until I had to.

The mood in the car is much lighter today, and it feels like we get through Georgia rather quickly. Maybe it's because we listen to music and don't fight. I'm lost in thought for a while, adding license plates. Somewhere between the edge of The Peach State and South Carolina, Cline and I both fall asleep, and Elliot has to fend for himself. I wake up a couple of times when we hit the odd pot hole, and I glance up to see him focused intently on the road, so I drift back off.

Not far from my grandmother's house, we are all awake, hopped up on sugar and hot boiled peanuts as I dole out an impossible game of Hump, Marry, and Kill.

"Cline, you're up next. Ready?" I turn in my seat and survey his face as he groans and frowns.

"Your choices blow," he complains.

"They are scientifically chosen. I'm not just throwing any old name out there for you to choose. Here are your choices: Matt Dylan, Dylan McDermott, Dermot Mulroney, and Rooney Mara."

"Bite me," he responds.

Elliot shoots me a grin and laughs silently as he grips the wheel tighter.

"Fine! Fine. Let's do this. Anna Kendrick …" I offer.

Cline perks up. "Yeah?"

"Kendrick Lamar. Lamar Odom."

"I hate you with the fire of a thousand suns," Cline says.

"You flatter me so, Cline Somers. You really do." I blow him a kiss. He, in turn, pretends to catch it and rolls down the window to throw it away.

The car begins to slow, and all joy slowly fades from my body as if I can feel it leaking out of my veins through my fingertips into the open air. Ruth Dewitt's mini mansion comes into view, and Elliot almost brings the car to a complete stop as he faces me.

I move my hand to tell him to keep moving forward. "Don't look so shocked. This is it. You're in the right driveway. Go ahead and pull up and then just go around the loop and park on the left where you see the other cars. I think that's where the maids and other people park." I don't know this for sure, but it seems like the most logical explanation, because there are old Hondas and a Toyota Tercel sitting there today.

I know that's not what Ruth would drive. If she drives herself at all.

"We should have dressed nicer," Cline says from the backseat.

"She won't let us inside. I don't think it will matter." I tell him quietly.

Elliot parks as I've instructed and turns to look at me. "Do you even have a plan? What are you going to do if she doesn't let you in?"

I run my fingers through my hair and wipe at

the mascara under my eyes, hoping I haven't smeared anything. "She's a lady. The least she could do is let me use the bathroom."

"Powder room. Say powder room. Be *fancy*." Cline is leaning across the console now so he can look up at the top of the house through the windshield. "Holy shit. Too bad she hates your guts."

"Yep." I grab my purse and exit the car. Once outside, I rummage around and find the flowered bag within, locate the correct orange bottle, pop the top and slip a yellow pill onto my tongue quickly, then swallow. I should have done it at least twenty minutes ago, but I wasn't expecting to be this overwhelmed.

Too late now.

The place is huge. Fountain out front in the circular driveway. Full staircase leading to the wraparound porch. Two stories with pillars running the length of both. It's essentially the cover of a V.C. Andrews book without the seduced cousin staring out of the upper window in a rainstorm.

I count my steps on the driveway and then count the stairs on the way up. There are no creaking boards as I cross the porch, and once I make it to the door, I pause. I can't believe I've actually made it this far. I know I'm crazy, but this is legitimately insane. I should have called Cara first. There is a moment of hesitation where I think maybe I should walk away, but before my brain can stop my hand, it's raised, and my finger is pressing the doorbell. There's a booming bell chiming throughout the expanse of the house.

My instinct is to run, but my feet are firmly planted as if they're glued to these white-painted wooden planks.

A voice inside my head is assuring me that she won't be the one to answer the door. Surely she has a person for that type of thing. It would be too low of her to open the door for—

"Can I help you?"

I take a step back under her scrutiny. She's smaller than I imagined, as I've built her up to be a larger-than-life evil villain in my head. We're about the same height, give or take the three inches of silver hair she has elegantly piled atop her head. She's dressed formally like she's about to attend an early dinner.

My voice is gone.

Her eyes narrow, and she takes a step back, her slipper-covered feet not making a sound as the floral skirt of her dress sways around her ankles. All I see is a bunch of green.

"Ruth Dewitt?" It's all I can manage before she shuts the door in my face.

It cracks back open again, and she purses her lips. "Yes. Again, can I help you?"

"I'm sorry. I'm so overwhelmed. I can't remember the last time I saw you. It's me. Audrey." There's a strange ringing in my ears, and the tips of them have gone red hot. I can't feel the ends of my fingertips.

Her posture goes rigid, and her face pales as she takes me in with one long look. "Please leave my property."

"Grandma—"

"Don't."

"I'm sorry. I apologize. Look, I know you don't want anything to do with me, and I can live with that. Really. But I'm twenty one now, and I just want to know about my mom. Patrick doesn't ever talk about her, and I don't know *anything*. You're the only person who I thought could possibly give me any information on her. What she was like. Who she was." My voice cracks and I try to tuck away the bit of desperation I'm starting to show.

"She was a wonderful daughter until she met your father. And then she died."

I close my eyes when she says it, because I know what she's implying. "I'm sorry. Would you please just give me five minutes of your time?"

Ruth's eyes flick to a huge grandfather clock standing in the hallway to my right, just in my line of vision. "I have a dinner. Today is not a good day."

I nod. "I understand. I did come a very long way, though. Would you mind if I used your powder room?"

The look of distrust in her eyes would destroy anyone else, but I've experienced much worse. And I'm simply putting on a show to gain entry into this house. Stooping to conquer, if you will. She only nods the slightest bit and then moves out of the way to let me pass.

"You'll have to use the one upstairs. The one down here is being renovated."

I take the stairs two at a time and locate the one she has mentioned, turn on the light and fan, close the door, and step back out into the hallway. There are multiple doors on each side of the hall, and I tentatively open each one, hoping not to make a sound as I try to figure out which room used to be my mother's. It's nerve wracking trying to be quiet, keeping my footsteps light, listening out for her to come barreling down the hallway, calling me a heathen and throwing holy water at me.

I'm disheartened each time a door reveals another room that is nothing more than a guest room, an office, or storage. And then I see it—the last room at the very end of the hallway. Opening it is like stepping back in time. The walls are a faded yellow wallpaper with little embossed canaries all over it. The bedspread has massive flowers embroidered everywhere, and a crocheted blanket of contrasting colors hangs off the side of four-poster bed. Framed concert posters adorn the wall, and pictures are tacked up on corkboard that's aging and missing chunks.

There's a suede fringed purse hanging from the back of her closet, a flower wreath sticking out of its pocket. I reach out to pull it down, and the closet door eases open enough for me to see plastic containers stacked inside the closet, arranged one on top of the other. All of them labeled: Wendy.

Wendy's pictures.

Wendy's drawings.

Wendy's school papers.

Wendy's books.

Wendy's medical records.

I have no idea how long I've been in here. There's no telling how much longer Ruth will buy me being in that bathroom. But I've just been handed a key to my mother's entire existence, and I'm not about pass it up. I quickly open the one with the pictures first and grab a stack blindly, shoving them down into the purse I've now claimed as my own. I bypass the drawings and papers, and I'm about to move beyond the books to the medical records when I notice that the books in question aren't *reading* books they're journals. They're *diaries*. With speed I can only assume is fueled by adrenaline, I jerk that drawer open and grab all of them, shoving them into the purse as well.

I'm just about to open the container holding the medical records when I hear my name being called. My heart lodges into my throat, realizing I've been caught. Ruth is banging on the bathroom door, and I jump to my feet, knocking over one of the bins in the process, sending a whole box of book reports scattering across my mom's old bedroom floor.

The commotion sends Ruth running in the direction of the bedroom, and in a moment of panic, I lunge for the double windows and throw them open. Running out onto the balcony that my mother probably once stood upon, I debate whether or not to run or stay. I sling her purse over one shoulder then mine over the other and crawl over the railing.

It's a short fall, but my life flashes before my eyes anyway, and I lose my breath upon impact. When I come to a few moments later, I am on the ground staring up at Ruth Dewitt shouting at me from the balcony that I'm from the devil, and I need to be cleansed of my sins. She's calling for an exorcism. She's practically screaming for a healing from my wicked ways.

All I can focus on are the purses bouncing at my sides as I round the corner of her house and wave my hands frantically while shouting for Elliot to start the car, because I'm one hundred percent sure she's about to call the police.

Elliot

Nags Head beach stretches out to my right, and the long pier extends into the waves on my left. Cline is out somewhere in town getting food, and Audrey sits between a couple of dunes as the sun begins to set in the sky The salt water carries in the wind, and I can feel it start to clump in my hair as I walk the edge of the shoreline, waiting.

I just have no idea what I'm waiting for.

She came tearing out of Ruth's backyard,

screaming for us to drive like she was in some kind of bank heist and had half a million dollars' worth of jewels in her possession. The pure excitement and fear on her face made my heart slam into my sternum, and Cline started swearing, and then, suddenly, she was in the car and the front door was open, and there was yelling and I was driving. Tires squealing. I slammed my head into the top of the car. Cline went flying across the backseat and almost into the back of the Xterra. But all the while, Audrey just held onto the oh-shit handle, a huge smile on her face, and her other arm gripping onto an old bag full of what I now know is a bunch of journals and pictures of her mom.

She's been in the dunes for over an hour looking through them, and while she's calmed down, she hasn't spoken at all, and I'm not sure if I'm supposed to approach her or not. This is what we came for. We figured the beach was the best place to go, so we headed that way, and I've been on the edge of the water ever since, hoping the cops don't show up. They haven't yet.

Audrey's face is downcast, partly hidden behind the tall grasses in the dunes and the shadows that are starting to form as the sun sets. Her skin glows orange from the distant burning of the last rays of the sun, and I take in her posture as she sits cross legged and shoeless in the sand. Her long black skirt is bunched up over her knees and covered in soft white sand, her teal v-neck t-shirt hangs open as she reads over the books scattered around her. I've walked closer and am staring, like I do. It's a thing my mom says I've done my entire life: I'm a people watcher.

It's probably why I'm good at making molds and creatures, characters and profiles for games. I catch the subtle things about people that others might just overlook or discount. I store them away, because the little things are what make up the whole of a person.

This girl pulls at her clothes unconsciously, especially around her stomach, like she's never exactly comfortable in her own skin. She's wearing a bracelet made of soda can tops and elastic today, and as she reads, she alternates between tucking her hair behind her ears and fussing with the aluminum against her skin. She's always moving.

"Hey, girl," I say as I approach and watch her jump slightly, her head rolling upward to acknowledge me. "Are you from Tennessee?"

She laughs and shakes her head, then closes the journal in her lap and stretches her legs out, letting her skirt fold down a little as she points her toes out. She pats the sand next to her and then wipes her hands off on her knees. "Am I the only ten you see, Elliot?"

"Damnit, you beat me to it." I sit down next to her and pull my knees to my chest, resting my arms on top of them as I gaze out at the ocean and the last remnants of the sunset.

"There aren't that many girls on the beach tonight, so I don't have much competition anyway," she says with a laugh. Her posture straightens and she holds up the book. "My mom was a badass, Elliot. These first diaries, or whatever, were from when she was super young, like, grade school and middle school. So they're mostly about friends and stupid shit. A few mentions of Ruth and her being too strict. Nothing really important. But then I got to these …"

I turn to look at the ones she's pointing to, and she runs her hand over the top of the stack. There are four full journals in the sand and another in her hand. Her eyes are wide, and the breeze from the sea lifts her hair from behind her ears, making it stick out from the side of her head and flutter in the wind. I reach out and tuck it back in and she doesn't flinch, just stares at me from a few inches away.

"These are from when she was in high school and things got rough at home, I guess. I mean I haven't read through all of them, and Ruth said my mom was a good daughter before she met my dad, but this says the opposite. My mom ran away and hitchhiked across a bunch of states before she met

Patrick. That's how they got together. She was on her way to a concert." She smiles so big, and I can see her eyes start to water before she turns her head and tries to be discreet about wiping at them. She clears her throat and looks back across the water. "Anyway. She went from here to Tennessee according to these. But nothing mentions another guy. Plus, these are all dated at the time she met Patrick, and I wasn't born for another fifteen years."

"This was about finding out who your mom was, right? Not the guy."

She doesn't look at me, just messes with her bracelet again and nods. "Yeah. I wanted to know my mom. That's all. And this is perfect. We can head back whenever you're ready. I got what I needed."

There's something in the way that she says it that makes me hesitate. "Where did she go first?"

Audrey turns to me, her upper body angled at mine and her eyebrows drawn together, mouth pulled into a frown. "Not far. She spent the first night here, actually. On the beach. Sleeping under the stars. Complained about the sand lice and stuff in the morning." She laughs and puts the book down in the sand. "Obviously, sleeping on the beach is illegal and you can get arrested for it, so it's a good thing she didn't try to do it now."

I shrug. "Or we could. *We* could sleep here tonight. Then go where she went next."

"You want to follow my mom's trail? You don't have to do that. That would be weird."

"Why?" I reach out and stop her from touching the metal around her wrist, holding her fingers between mine. She goes still as we both look down at where we're touching, and I glance up just as the sun slips beyond the horizon. "When you called that night and we went to the diner, you said you wanted to run away. Maybe it's in your DNA. Maybe you need to. Just like your mom."

"There's a lot of stuff in my DNA. Doesn't mean I should just go off and do whatever." She snatches her hand away from mine and stands quickly, gathering up the books and reaches for her shoes. "It's all nice in theory, but …"

I stand too and take a step back to watch her wage a war within herself as she weighs the options I've presented. "But, what? Come on. Run away with me, Audrey."

Her stare is unwavering as she chews on her lip. "And Cline. Unless you plan to leave him here."

It deflates the situation a little bit, but I don't care. "And Cline. It'll be fun. Let's go where your mom went. We'll start with tonight. Are you in?"

Her hand slips into mine, and it's the only answer I need.

"We're gonna get caught and go to jail and die." Cline is whispering from the backseat like we're on a stakeout.

"You can speak in a normal voice. We're inside the car." Audrey is pretending not to be nervous, but the waver in her voice belies her false bravado. "Also, that's not how it works. You don't just go to jail and die. If anything, it would be a holding cell and your mom would have to come bail you out. You'd pee in front of a few guys. Like on TV."

"That's how I would die. I'd hold my pee until it retracted back into my body and I died of sepsis." Cline hisses the last *s* at her.

It's nearly midnight, and we've seen a couple patrol cars ride by as well as a local with a flashlight looking for crap left on the beach. But I'm bound and determined to do this simply because it almost feels like we can't stop now. I didn't drive all the way to Alabama to get my dad's old camping gear and then into North Carolina to steal books from an old lady's house just to stop now.

We wait another fifteen minutes, and once we're sure everything is clear, I make a motion with my fingers in the dark. Audrey leans over the console and slaps my hand.

"The hell are you doing? This isn't some kind

of Black Ops mission. Plus, the sleeping bags are in the back, so we have to open the car doors and stuff."

"For once I agree with her. Don't be a douche." Cline reaches behind him and wrestles with a sleeping bag before sliding it forward and pushing it between the seats. "Here. Wait. Are there only two bags?"

I look over my shoulder at him and raise my hands in question. "Did you not bring one? What did you pack?"

"I packed clothes! And snacks. A phone charger. My pillow. I thought we'd be sleeping in the car or a hotel or something. Don't give me that look, Elliot. I wasn't exactly invited."

"Then you don't exactly have a sleeping bag," I counter.

Audrey sighs and rubs her face with her hands. "He can have mine."

"What are you going to sleep in?" I'm all for chivalry, but I was kind of counting on having something to sleep in tonight, and I'm sure Cline won't reject her offer which means I'll give her mine and be left without.

She grins in the darkness. "Jet pack time in a sleeping bag?"

My mouth drops open, and I slide away from her to the car door. "What kind of heathen do you think I am?"

"We brought an extra blanket. Relax. I'll give you space. Jeez." The look in her eyes tells me she's lying.

Cline opens the door and starts to scoot outside. "I don't even want to know what kind of weird-ass code that is."

We all meet at the front of the car and wait to see if anyone is around. When I'm sure the coast is clear, I whisper for them to run, and we all take off at the same time, headed straight for the dunes, white sand spraying up around our feet as we dash toward a dip in the beach. The light doesn't shine as bright there, and a fence blocks the area off just enough that if we're sleeping on the ground, it would be hard for anyone to see us.

Breathing heavy and laughing quietly, we slip off our shoes and unroll the sleeping bags. Cline is in his quickly while Audrey and I unzip ours and open it to flatten it out on the moonlit sand. She lets the blanket unfurl, and the wind from the ocean makes it fly out of her hand, so I catch it and bring it back, settling it over us as we lay on our backs beneath the stars.

She stares up at the sky, her chin jutting out from the edge of the blanket and her eyes reflecting the clear constellations above. I wonder for a moment what she's thinking. If she's glad that she's here. If I made the right choice. When her hand finds mine between us and she smiles as she closes her eyes, I have to believe that she's thinking about her mom and that I did the right thing after all.

Audrey

I can't sleep at all lying between Elliot and Cline on the beach under the same stars my mom once slept beneath. My mind races, and my chest is heavy with so many questions that I can't calm myself down enough to even allow a minutes' worth of rest. The moment I close my eyes, I'm assaulted with things I've done wrong or something I've said that I shouldn't have. Year's worth of anxiety plague me in the darkness. Miranda's face flashes between childhood memories that I once held sacred, and they become marred with her presence even though she wasn't there.

My thoughts turn to her and her increasing hatred of me throughout the years. I wonder exactly when she was told about Patrick not being my father. I wonder what the precise moment was when she stopped hating me for having his attention and started loathing me for being born at all. Her transition from cold step-mother to functioning alcoholic, pill-popping antagonizer didn't happen overnight. It was gradual.

Her girls' nights out became more often, bleeding into weekdays. She'd find any excuse to take a pill. Burn her finger on the stove? Pop an OxyContin. Headache from the night before? Take a Vicodin. She had multiple doctors and multiple prescriptions, a mini pharmacy in her bathroom that Patrick overlooked for one reason or another. Lorcet, Percocet, Demerol, and I think one time I found a bottle of Adderall stashed away in there.

When she was prescribed the Xanax on top of all of that is when things started to really get bad.

My incident had already occurred, and she knew I was in therapy. She'd been the one to find me, and some nights when I can't sleep I wonder why she didn't just leave me there. Her life would have been so much easier if she had. But a diagnosis of depression and anxiety at a young age will color a person's perception of you. She didn't side step me and treat me like I was fragile. No, she seemed to come at me harder, like maybe I was just a little cracked and she could fully break me.

Patrick tiptoed around me, ever watchful when he was in the room. But I didn't say anything to him about what was happening behind his back in his own home. Would he even believe me? Or would he say I was crazy and take her side anyway? It wasn't worth the risk.

The weight gain from the meds came on quickly and so did Miranda's ridicule. I'd stopped speaking to everyone after what I'd done. Dr. Stark once asked me if I was embarrassed by it, but I stand firm that I'm not. No one knows except the three of us and the doctors. I stopped talking because everyone I ever knew in my entire life knew *Byrdie* and she technically didn't exist. How do you talk to people who don't even know the real you … when *you* don't even know who you truly are?

The silence was first. Then the weight. Miranda put me on this really strict vegetarian diet that she would prepare. Then she went on Atkins and would sit across from me, eating a pound of bacon in the morning, laughing as she stuffed her face. Patrick never saw.

Holidays meant nothing to me anymore. The last few that happened while I lived in that house, they travelled on their own, saying they needed more time together. I pretended to understand. Acted like I didn't care. I was a teenager and didn't want to be around them anyway.

Miranda's mother called often and would send gifts but had nothing to do with me. Once, right before Christmas, as Patrick was in the kitchen getting coffee, Miranda held up a pair of diamond earrings her mother had bought her and sighed. "When you see things like this, does it make you miss having a mom?" she asked, the lights from the tree reflected in her too small eyes, like she was innocently posing a question that wasn't going to send me into an anxiety attack right there on the spot.

I spent the rest of the day wedged between my bed and my dresser grasping for a reason to live.

Panic rises in my chest as the memories begin to bombard me, so I slip out of the blanket and move toward the shoreline as the sky begins to grow a bit brighter. I've never seen a sunrise over the ocean before, so I set my eyes on that as I count my breaths and swallow down the swelling in my throat. Fingers pressed to my pulse point, I stretch my other hand out and tap out a rhythm of threes and fours until I've calmed myself enough to start taking in air. The tears that have collected in my eyes begin to spill down my cheeks and are instantly swept away by the breeze coming off the oncoming waves.

It's moments like these that remind me that no matter how hard I try or how many things I do, my life will never be easy or what other people consider conventional. I may fight this thing until the day I die. *But at least I'll fight it.*

The thing that's beginning to worry me is that my mother's journals show no sign of this being hereditary.

Nagging thoughts of this plague me as I shuffle back to where the boys are still sleeping in the sand. Cline's snoring is so loud I'm afraid he could set off a car alarm. But Elliot is resting on his side, his arm outstretched toward my pillow like he's been searching for me in his sleep. My chest aches at the sight, so I look away, reminding myself that we're all here as friends, on a mission to find answers for the sole reason of getting info on me for Elliot's game. And along the way, I will find the courage to talk to Cline. Then I can go about my life, and Dr.

Stark can get off my back about this little Eight Steps to Happiness bullshit she's been pushing at me for the last year.

Elliot stirs and his eyes blink open once, then twice, before he sits up and holds a hand to his forehead to shield his face from the sunrise. "Hey."

"Can I have your keys?" I reach out my hand like I've casually been waiting for him to wake up.

He digs in his pocket and holds them out to me, and I take them quickly. "You might want to wake up The Beast over there. I'm sure they'll start patrolling once the sun is up. We should get outta here." I give a quick nod and rush as fast as I can through the sand toward his car. Given the short amount of time I have, I open the passenger door and struggle to pull my purse from beneath the seat where I had it stashed away just in case anyone looked inside the windows overnight.

With shaking fingers, I locate the flower-printed bag and pull out my array of bottles. With precision I've perfected over the years, I take the tops off of them one at a time and replace them quickly before moving onto the next. Five bottles in all in the morning. The pills are all lined up along the car seat as I step around the back to grab a water bottle from the trunk, and when I turn to walk back to where the passenger door is open, Elliot is standing there, staring at my line of prescriptions.

His eyes hold no judgment as they meet mine. "How many of those do you take?"

I push down the fear of what he could possibly be thinking about me as I move to stand by him and then angle myself in front to scoop the pills into my hand. They all go into my mouth at once, and I have them swallowed with one gulp of water from the bottle. Facing him, I give the best smile I can manage. "Not enough to get full. We should get breakfast. Is Cline up?"

"I got a campsite for us at Devil's Fork, but we have

to stay for a minimum of two nights. I told them two was fine." Elliot pockets his phone as he gets back into the car. The rest stop isn't packed, but there are enough people around that sitting in the car has kept me entertained while the boys have been doing their business.

"I'll pay you back for the campsite," I say, and I mean it. I've never expected anything from anyone.

Elliot smiles and starts the car, the beauty mark next to his ear raising a little in the process. "Just fill up the next tank and we'll be even."

Cline rushes across the parking lot, still zipping his pants, practically tripping over himself before he launches his large body into the car. "I got tapped."

"What?" I turn in my seat to look at his face and he's gone almost completely white, sweat beads trickling from beneath his stupid hat.

"I was taking a shit and the guy next to me tapped my foot. He TAPPED MY FOOT."

"Maybe he just had a wide spread," Elliot offers as he begins to reverse out of the parking lot.

"Maybe there was a glory hole in the wall that I was unaware of. Don't act like you don't know about *the tap* at rest stops." He slides sideways and rests his head on the pillow he has in the backseat, tipping his hat forward in the process. He's breathing heavy, and his cheeks are bright red, but after about a full minute of silence he shrugs and pulls out his phone. "I don't really blame him, though. I mean ... look at me. I'm ridiculously good looking."

I start to say something, but Elliot's hand on my knee stops me. He has a wry grin on his face and closes his eyes for a second while he shakes his head like I should just leave it. So I do. Because I trust this boy and I have no idea why.

Devil's Fork is, in a word, gorgeous. The campsite is small and on the water, close enough to the bathrooms that I could find them without a flashlight, but far enough away that I don't smell them being downwind. Lake Jacosse spreads out before us, peaceful and astoundingly clear. I'm on the edge of the water, taking in how different this is from the ocean we were just staring at around six hours ago. The boys are setting up the eight man tent directly behind me, and there's another small popup tent to my left that looks empty at the moment, leaving my mind to wonder about its inhabitants.

"Where is this rock that your mom jumped off of?" Cline calls from his lazy stance, holding one of the rods while Elliot threads it through the loops at the base of the tent.

I shrug and point off into the distance. "We need a way to get over there to the waterfall." Wendy's diary says that she snuck into the park after hours and found a group of people her age sitting around drinking and just asked if she could stay with them. They were the ones with the boat. Her entire rebellion hinged on the fact that people weren't going to *murder* her.

My once-best-friend comes to stand next to me and crosses his arm, his large frame blocking out the sunlight coming through the trees. "Do we have a boat?"

"No."

"Were you planning on getting a boat?"

"There are ways."

He nods in my periphery and sighs like he's about to say something really shitty when the water at our feet begins to ripple and wave, coming in at rougher intervals, and then we hear the sound of a boat drop into a lower gear. I think we both see her at the same time. She's golden-tan, raven haired, and wearing one of the smallest pink bikinis I've seen in a really long time. That's saying something, because my bedroom has a view of one of the student apartment pools off campus.

The wind is making her hair fly everywhere, and she lifts her sunglasses to the top of her head to secure her tresses like a headband then offers a friendly smile and wave as she continues on to the dock to our left.

Cline is speechless as I look up at his face, suppressing the urge to reach over and close his mouth for him.

"Did your entire life just flash before your eyes? Wedding, babies, white picket fence?" I ask and hold back a smile as he blinks his way back into reality.

"What? No. It was more like topless, in a tent, on her back."

"You're disgusting."

His eyes meet mine and he holds my gaze as he speaks the next words so that they'll hit me straight in the gut. "Every guy does it. Ask Elliot how many times he's closed his eyes and pictured you naked recently."

I turn and walk away before he says anything else, my throat suddenly tight and stomach twisted with worry. It's possible he's right, but it doesn't mean anything. It doesn't have to mean anything.

The bathroom looms before me, and I hurry inside like it's my only safe place, some sort of dirty salvation in the woods where I can have some peace and quiet. But I know better, because no matter how far I run, I can never outrun myself. I have the loudest voice I know, even when I'm completely silent.

The ocean's salt is still sticking to me, and there's sand in between my toes when I walk into one of the stalls. I stand there for a minute, trying to breathe through my nose and form a plan on how we'll get out to the rocks so that I can jump like Wendy had. So I can feel the exhilaration of the drop into the water. She talked about the freedom of the fall, and even though I'm terrified of heights, I would do this in her honor. Just to feel a flicker of what she might have experienced.

There's a creak and then the sound of the main door being slammed shut. A shuffling of feet through the water on the floor alerts me to someone else in the bathroom, and just when I start to hold my breath and my heartbeat gets louder in my ears,

I hear the click clack of flip flops on the floor, and I know it's not one of the guys coming to find me. It's another camper.

Of course it is.

I exhale and turn around, lifting my foot to flush the toilet so I don't seem like some kind of weirdo, and let the commode noise die down before I reach for the door handle. There's a huge colorful butterfly sculpture attached to the yellowed tile up by the screened windows, and I pause for a moment, wondering who would put that much effort into decorating a restroom before the sound of the other person washing their hands brings me back to reality.

Gaining my composure, I step out and head toward the sinks when I notice that the other occupant of the bathroom is the girl from the boat. She's got a towel wrapped around her chest, her hair thrown into a ponytail, and her sunglasses perched on top of her head again. She smiles at me from the mirror's reflection.

"Hi."

"Hey," I say and turn the water on to wash nothing from my hands. When I'm done, I reach for a paper towel, but she hands me one instead.

"September."

"What?" I ask, leaning back to look her over. Her cheeks are sunburnt, and her bright green eyes are a little red so I'm wondering if she's high or if it's the lake water.

"I'm September. What's your name?" She extends a slender hand my way, and I blush as I realize that she's just being nice and that this is probably how my mom did shit back in the day. Just talked to people. It takes a few drinks for me to get this friendly. This girl is offering up her hand like she's ready to be best friends.

"Audrey. I saw you come by on your boat."

She grins. "It's a rental. I've only got it for another day. Are you in the lot next to the little red tent?"

"Yeah, how did you know?"

"We're neighbors for a couple more nights." She turns to her reflection in the mirror again and presses the pink spots beneath her eyes. "These are gonna hurt like a bitch once the sun goes down. I probably won't get any sleep at all."

"One of the guys I'm with snores like an eighty-year-old man who forgot to plug in his CPAP machine, so you probably won't get any sleep anyway. My apologies in advance."

Her laugh is loud and genuine, and her smile reflects in her eyes. But the sound also bounces all along the walls, across the tile, and with it comes the sound of fluttering.

"What the hell?" Her eyebrows draw together as she looks around. "Did you hear that?"

"Maybe it's a bird in the rafters?" I strain to look up into the darkened ceiling.

"No. That wasn't a bird." She steps forward and pushes open one of the stalls and we both peek in to see if there's anything there.

"That's weird," I say as the door slams shut,

rattling the other stalls.

She turns to me with wide eyes. "What's weird?"

"There wasn't a butterfly statue in that one."

"What. The. Fuck …"

The reverberation of the doors reaches the last stall where I was standing and we hear the sound again, this time more urgent than before, and faster than a scream can leave my mouth, that thing that was in the stall with me rises and takes flight right above our heads.

"That's a fucking moth, Audrey!" September is screaming and it's making the thing go crazy. It's three feet tall, I swear, and it has no sense of personal space, because it's flying at us intermittently as we are screaming and covering our heads.

"I thought it was art!" I'm ducking and weaving, trying to make it to the door and she's right behind me, slipping through old water, and Mothra is getting more agitated by the second. I reach the door, throw it open, and we both run screaming out into the open air, crouched low as the beast with wings follows us out and pivots up and over the bathhouse.

Cline and Elliot are running full speed toward us, and I've never been so happy to see someone before in my entire life. Elliot has his arms out and I grab him hard, practically jumping into his arms and wrap myself like a sloth around his body.

September is brushing dirt from her knees, and her towel has fallen away, and I watch as Cline stoops to pick it up for her. From the corner of my eye I see them make eye contact for the first time and something inside me stirs. An unraveling of rope around my heart. A thread that was knotted begins to loosen and fray.

I press my face into Elliot's neck and smile, squeezing him a little tighter. "That's September. She's our neighbor. She has a boat."

Elliot

My laptop is plugged into a charger inside the car, and I'm trying to catch up on some lost time I should have been dedicating to the game instead of this impromptu road trip. I'm easily distracted by the camp fire and Cline's new fascination with September. My attention also drifts to Audrey's attempt to stay out of their way while they set up stuff for dinner.

She hovers just out of their general vicinity,

closer to the tent until one of them walks over to get something from the cooler, then she does a quick turn and finds something else to do. It's an awkward dance that's keeping me from concentrating on the task in my lap.

"Audrey," I yell to her, and she stops cold, turning to look at me like a deer caught in headlights. "Come here." I motion for her to sit by me in the trunk and notice when her shoulders visibly relax as she makes her way across the gravel to the back of the car. The tires bounce a bit as she climbs in and folds her legs beneath her, plastering a smile on her face to hide whatever tension she just had displayed out there.

"Are you on a deadline?" she asks, craning her neck to look at my screen.

"Kind of. They want my first pitch soon, so I need to have something for them or else I'll blow it before I even have a chance to show them my entire idea."

Her focus drifts across the fire toward Cline

and September, so I close my laptop and angle to face her better. "I've never seen him like this before. I mean, I've watched him hit on girls and take them back to our place or whatever—like what happened at your party—but he's actually talking to her. Listening and paying attention. I guess there's a first time for everything." I keep my tone light, hoping to get her to talk, because she's being so quiet.

"It's not the first time," she says softly, her stare unwavering.

"No?"

"No. I never believed in love at first sight until sixth grade. We got this new student on the first day of school and Cline got this look on his face like his entire world had just suddenly changed in the blink of an eye. She was all he talked about for a week before he got the guts to ask her out at lunch. He did it with a note, because he didn't want to be embarrassed if she said no. Which she did."

Her eyes meet mine and there's a sadness in the way her mouth is pulled so tight and how her eyes are narrowed. "She didn't have to be such a total bitch about it, though. Showed everybody the note. Made him feel like an asshole for it. Like she was better than him."

"Oh." It's really all I can say, because we're twenty-one now, and that kind of stuff doesn't matter anymore in the grand scheme of things. I doubt Cline even remembers it. But Audrey's sitting here like she's reliving it all over again for the first time.

"Told you I hated a girl named Kelsey once." She smiles and shakes my shoulder roughly. "I stole her bra in P.E. She had to run a mile holding her boobs. Low key revenge for my best friend? Worth it."

There are suddenly so many questions I want to ask. Like, how things could be that close between the two of them and then suddenly one day they were strangers who hated each other with no reason whatsoever. Was it a misunderstanding? Why had Audrey run away in the first place?

Before I can speak, Cline's calling out that dinner is ready, and Audrey is out of the car holding out her hand for me to follow. So I do. The four of us sit in front of the fire with hotdogs on wires, trying to get them cooked and not burnt, but Cline keeps putting his too far into the flames, and he's caught three consecutive wieners on fire.

"Don't put it in so far," September chides him, and he makes eye contact with me, his eyes wide and mouth open like he wants to make a dirty joke and it's killing him not to.

I swallow my bite quickly to cut him off before he can do something stupid and say, "September is a really unique name. Did your parents name you after the month you were born?"

The pretty brunette turns and rolls her eyes like she's heard this a hundred times and shakes her head. Her hair is pulled back into a wild ponytail, and the fire makes the right side of her face glow bright orange as the flames pop and crackle. "I was born in July. And no, September is not the month I was conceived, either. There's no logic to it."

There's a choking sound from my left and Audrey turns her head when I look over at her. She's wiping her mouth and covering it with her hand as her shoulders start to shake. Turning back to look at September, I note that her eyes are squinted in amusement.

"My sister's name is Thursday. Guess when she was born?" She asks, pointing her hot dog in my direction.

"On a Thursday?" I guess.

"On a Monday," she answers with a laugh.

Cline is really trying to keep it together because he likes this girl, but I can hear his voice crack when he asks the next question. "So do you only have the one sister?"

"No, I have a brother, too." Her face is expressionless as she waits for one of us to ask what we all want to know.

"What month or day did they name him after?" Cline can hardly get the question out.

"They named him Anderson. He got off easy."

She takes a bite of her food and grins. "I tried to go by my middle name for a while, Jocelyn. But then people wanted to give me a nickname, and it was Jocie, but that turned into Jockey, and eventually it was easier just to go back to being September Worley. No one wants to abbreviate that name. And even if I have to explain that my parents just like to mess with people by naming us weird names, it's still mine, ya know?"

"So, why are you only staying through tomorrow night? And why are you alone?" Audrey scoots closer to me so that the other girl can hear her.

September is very serious when she answers. "I've come to the end of my journey. My time of Rumspringa is over and I must return home."

Cline's entire wire, hot dog and all, goes directly into the fire. "Oh, my god … sorry, I'm sorry. You're Amish? How? And you only have a few days left? You're going back? I—you—this—"

September breaks and starts laughing, bent over, her hand raised toward him as she waves it frantically for him to stop stuttering. "Stop! Stop. I'm kidding. Holy shit, your face. I wish you could have seen your face. Are you okay? Oh, wow. Did that freak you out?"

He's crestfallen as he tries to collect himself and rummages around for another hot dog and bun. "No, it didn't freak me out." I know for a fact it didn't. He watches those Amish shows on TV all the time, and I'm a thousand percent sure he's got a thing for one of the girls on there.

"I'm finishing my gap year and headed back home. I took the time off to decide if I wanted to get my master's or not." Her voice is gentle now as she reaches out and pats his knee. He looks up, and his eyes get big when her hand makes contact.

"What are you studying?" Audrey asks.

September looks beyond me to answer. "Clinical Psychology."

Audrey's fingers slip around my bicep, and she grips harder than I think she realizes when she answers in that fake voice she reserves for Cline,

"That's amazing."

The tent is quiet as the sun begins to peek in through the window screen facing the east. Audrey's body is pressed up against mine, her face buried in my chest, only the top of her head visible under the blanket. I shake her gently and she curls up even tighter.

"Today's the big day. You're jumping off a cliff. Are you ready?"

Her head raises slowly and her eyes appear, sleep rimmed and half open. "Did I tell you I'm afraid of heights?" I move to sit up, but she presses me back down with her hand on my face. "Don't move yet. I need to get into the right head space. Just stay here with me for a minute, okay?"

"Yeah, okay, I can do that." Wrapping an arm over her, I pull her closer and stare up at the top of the tent. The smell of the damp nylon takes me back to a memory of my dad, and I blink it away before the feeling can overwhelm me. I try not to dwell on thinking about him in any way other than with a detached eye through making my game. Or talking about him limitedly with my mom. Otherwise, the pain gets to be something I can't shake.

"Cline stayed with September last night?"

"Yeah." I laugh and it causes her head to bounce on my chest. "I told you he moves fast."

"Well, if it's any consolation to you, she asked if you were single."

I sit up and she follows, her hair sticking to the side of her face while she yanks her clothes into place. "Did you tell her yes?"

"Were you interested?" Her eyes are searching mine, and for a moment my heart beats off rhythm under her gaze. Would I have been interested in another girl right now? Hooking up with September in her tent with Audrey and Cline in the one I'd brought for us all on this trip? The thought of Audrey in the sleeping bag alone while …

Then there would have been the wrath of Cline.

"No. I wouldn't do that to Cline." *Or you*, I think, but I don't say it out loud.

Her demeanor has gone cold, and she scoots away to stand up. "Next time a girl asks if you're available, I'll let her know you are. I have to go change." With that, she's gone from the tent and I'm left to wonder exactly what the hell I've gotten myself into.

The sounds from the other campsite let me know our friends are awake, so I get up and change into my swim shorts and grab a towel, stepping out of the tent just in time to see Cline tumbling out of September's. She's on all fours, her head poking out of the flap, and he leans down to give her a kiss before he turns and half runs, half hops across gravel to get to me.

"I take it last night went well?"

The grin on his face is more than enough to answer my question, but he does anyway. "I wanna keep her. Can we keep her? Can she come with us?"

"She's not a puppy, dude. She's a person."

His whole face lights up. "I think she might be *my* person." He doesn't wait for a response from me before disappearing into the tent and making a bunch of noise while he changes into his swim shorts.

I start to think about what he's said. Is it that easy? Can you just meet someone that fast and know? Shouldn't it take longer?

As I'm pondering these questions, Audrey appears on her way back from the bathrooms. She has changed into a bathing suit, but she's wearing some sort of cover-up on top of it. Her hair is pulled back away from her face, no trace of makeup, and she's doing that thing with her hands again.

"Cline's in there," I call out in warning before she walks into the tent and finds him with his dick hanging out.

"Shit. I need my bag from in there." Her fingers are tapping faster now, and there's a look of panic that crosses her features momentarily before she smooths them out again.

"Which one?" I ask, though I think I know.

"The small one with the flowers. I keep it in my purse."

"I know the one. I'll grab it." She doesn't have time to argue with me before I'm unzipping the tent and crouching inside, ignoring my friend and his half naked ass. The bag is exactly where she says it will be, and it makes a rattling noise when I grab it, so I hold it closer to my stomach to quiet it down. Grabbing another towel, I wrap it inside and slip a bottle of water in there, too, before escaping back out without a word. I hand her the entire thing, discreetly packaged, because I know. And unlike what she may be used to, I'm not judging her.

Her lips are pressed together, and her cheeks are bright pink as she takes it from me with a quiet thank you. As she turns to walk away, I stop her and slip a granola bar on top of the towel. "Let me know if you need anything else."

Elliot

She's gone for twenty minutes, and in that time, September has changed, grabbed something to eat, and left with Cline for the boat. When Audrey returns, it's just the two of us and she's a little calmer, a little less edgy.

"They went to the dock to get the boat ready. I said we'd meet them there in a few," I tell her as she stops just outside the extinguished fire pit. "We can go whenever you're ready. No rush."

She's staring at me, holding all her stuff, still and unwavering. We're in a silent stand-off, neither of us moving.

"Why are you being so nice to me, Elliot?"

"What do you mean?" I ask, taking a step forward. She inches back a step and stops, staring at me curiously.

"Like, from the minute we met you've been nothing but nice to me. You haven't said a mean thing once. You haven't made me feel bad about myself. You don't say anything about *these*." She lifts her bag into the air and shakes it, making the bottles inside rattle. "You're willing to drive me places and let me sleep next to you. You come running when I'm getting attacked by people-sized moths. You do really nice shit for me for no reason at all. Why?"

"I don't know. Maybe my mom just raised me right?" I'm struggling to figure out why she's asking me why I'm just simply being a decent human being.

"You don't even really know anything about me. We're practically strangers."

"That's not true," I counter and take another step forward. "I think I know plenty about you. Enough to know that I like you. That you make me laugh, and I like being around you."

Her body stiffens and she huffs, walking forward to get by me and into the tent to put her stuff away. I follow, unsure of exactly what it is that's happening or what I'm supposed to say right now. "Are you freaking out about the jump or something? You're acting weird."

"Am I? Again, you don't really know me, so you don't have much to go off of, do you?" She's shoving her bags into the corner of the tent by her pillow, and I can see her hands shaking as she rises to her feet.

"If I don't know anything about you, then educate me. Because in case you haven't figured it out, I *want* to know you, Audrey. If I didn't, I wouldn't be here. I wouldn't have taken the time to drive your ass all the way out here and pushed you to do the shit your mom did so you could figure out whatever it is that you seem to be missing. If I'm not making myself clear, I'm not doing this for me. I'm doing this for *you*!"

She closes the gap between us faster than I can blink, before I can even take a breath, and she has her arms around my neck, pulling my face down to hers, pressing her mouth against mine. I'm stunned for a moment, and my reaction time is slow, because just a second before, I was filled with anger, but now Audrey has her body pressed against mine, and her tongue is tracing my lower lip. I've forgotten what I was even mad about in the first place.

I pull her tight, wrapping an arm around her back and leaning down to pick her up under her butt. She wraps her legs around my waist and kisses me deeper, a tiny moan escaping when I squeeze her closer. She's crushed against my chest, her little dress bunched up over her thighs, as I step forward and kneel down to lay her on her back atop the sleeping bag bed we've made our own for the last couple nights. Yanking from my back, she has my shirt up over my head and flung over to the side within seconds. Her hands roam my skin as she kisses me again, and I press into her touch, letting her fingertips skim and press, fingernails lightly scraping down my sides.

"I lied," she says breathlessly, pulling away to look between us and then leaning in to press a wet kiss to my neck.

"What?" I'm barely holding myself off of her, and the more she touches me the harder it's getting. Pun intended.

"When I told you in the diner that I don't find you attractive. I lied. Jesus, Elliot ..." The backs of her fingers sweep across my stomach and lower until they brush across the top of my swimming trunks, and I'm lost in my attempt at control. My hips dip forward, and I roll into her, my teeth nipping at the soft skin of her shoulder. The friction of sliding against her makes me squeeze my eyes shut and I exhale by her ear, gripping the sleeping bag at her sides.

Pushing up to my knees, I get better balance and find her mouth again. My hands roam her sides and push the fabric of her cover up higher until it's shoved under her breasts, and I break away from kissing her only long enough to help her lift up and discard it next to my shirt. The feel of her skin against my own, even with the material of her bathing suit between us, is making me feel off kilter in the best of ways.

I look at her face, and her cheeks are flushed pink, her eyes half lidded, lips parted and puffy. Audrey is a beautiful girl, but right now she's downright erotic. She cranes her neck higher when I lean down to kiss her there, her back arching and breasts pressing against my chest as she squirms beneath me. Her hands are in my hair, on my neck, tugging and pulling as I descend to her chest. She begins to shake when my mouth hovers above the swell of her left breast.

"Wait," she says quietly, and her grip on my hair tightens.

I go still and close my eyes, exhaling through my nose, dropping my forehead to her chest.

"I'm sorry. I'm just really …"

"What?" I ask, raising my head to look her in the eyes. She averts her gaze and then closes her eyes tightly.

"You said you wanted know something about me, right? Well … I don't really like how I look right now, so I'm kind of self-conscious about being naked around people."

I rest my chin on her chest and smile, waiting for her to open her eyes. "You don't like your body? That's what you want me to know?" She meets my gaze and frowns. "This body?" I run my right hand down her side and over her hip, settling her leg around my waist again as I press into her once more. "That's a shame, because I really, *really* like it. In case you couldn't tell."

She presses her lips together to stop from smiling, and her cheeks burn brighter.

I nudge her breast with my nose and kiss the skin below it, flicking my tongue out to taste my way across to the other side. She's soft and trembling beneath me as I leave a trail of kisses down her side and then across her stomach, stopping to look up from her belly button. "Look at this," I say and run my finger around her innie. "How could you hate this?" Her hands cover her face as she laughs, and I smile at the sound, shifting lower and kissing below the spot I was just touching. My tongue traces the top of her bikini bottoms, and her hands fall away from her face, finding the back of my head again.

I press my lips to the inside of her thigh and brush an open-mouthed kiss over where heat is rolling off of her. Making my way back up, I kiss her lips again, tracing her tongue with my own. With a flattened palm, I slide my hand down her stomach, and my fingers stop just above the elastic to her bathing suit bottoms. Her eyes open and hold contact with mine as I inch down the smallest bit. She holds her breath, and the tent is silent as her knees widen and allow my hand to slip beneath the fabric.

"You're beautiful, Audrey," I whisper, hoping she believes it as my fingers seek and explore. I hold her close and kiss her more, even when she begins to shake and whimper. Even when her legs jerk and she digs her short fingernails into my shoulder. Even when she clings to me and cries out my name and God's name and something else that may not be a real word, but makes me feel like a man anyway.

Her body goes limp, and she cradles my face in her hands as she stares at me, breathing heavy and shivering. "I'm going to ruin the mood here by say-ing this, but if you ever make a video game and your character needs a super power—what you just did should be it."

"Nope. Mood not ruined at all. Hard-on still intact. And ego boosted to a thousand percent," I say, chuckling then laying on my back and flexing my fingers.

Audrey rises up on shaky knees and leans over to give me another kiss. "Give me a second to recover, and I'm gonna repay you for that."

"Okay—"

"What the fuck is taking y'all so long?" Cline's voice cuts through the air like a bomb going off, and Audrey flies back like she's been physically hit, landing on her butt. She's covered in red marks, her chest bright pink, and hair a knotted disaster. I'm lying on my back with a raging boner, fingernail marks all over my back, and my hand curled into a fist.

We're so busted.

Cline's not speaking to either of us. The look on his face when we came out of the tent was enough to make my dick go soft in an instant. He didn't believe for a second that we hadn't had sex. It didn't matter that he had just told me that September was his soul mate. It didn't matter that he hated Audrey. No.

"Treason," is all he said before he turned and stalked off toward the boat.

We'd followed behind silently like two kids caught in the act by their parents. I wanted to reach over and grab her hand, take her to the side and tell her it was okay. Instead, we're dead silent as we walk.

September let Cline drive the boat, guiding him toward the waterfall and cliff that Audrey's mom had written about in her journal. I watched from a distance as Audrey sat at the front of the boat, her attention on the horizon, posture rigid, waiting for the falls to come into view. As soon as they did, she began fidgeting. Tugging at her hair and clothes. Tapping her fingers.

I cross the boat as we drop to a lower gear and go to sit by her side. "Hey, are you gonna be okay?"

She smiles like everything is just fine. "Of course. This is what we came for." Her fingers trace the marks on my shoulder and she winces. "I'm really sorry about that."

"I'm not," I respond, tucking a piece of wayward hair behind her ear.

September jumps from the side of the boat and pulls it to the shore with a rope and ties it off. The waves from our wake cause the boat to rock roughly, and Audrey slides into me, arms flailing. I catch her, and from the corner of my eye, I can see Cline shoot me a look. I flip him the bird in response.

The look of shock on his face is almost worth not getting off half an hour ago. Almost.

The girls are already off the boat and headed up to the cliff, but I stay behind and wait for my best friend, because even though he's being a shithead, he's still *my* shithead.

Cline takes his sweet-ass time doing absolutely nothing on the boat until he doesn't have anything else he can't *not* do anymore, and he's forced to get off. He's still not making eye contact with me, but that's his problem. It's not the first time I've experienced one of his tantrums. It's just the first time one's been directed at me.

"Exactly how long are you going to give me the Somers Silent Treatment?" I ask, keeping his pace up the trail.

He grunts instead of answering.

"You're still stuck in the car with us for at least another week. You know that, right?"

"Funny you should mention that. September said she could make a detour through Tennessee on her way back home. I figure since this trip is turning more into the Audrey and Elliot Show, I could just hitch a ride back with her. Leave you two to whatever it is that you're doing."

We've come to a clearing and can see the jumping point where the girls are standing. Audrey is crouched down, hugging her knees, and September is leaning over her, rubbing her back. My first instinct is to run to her, but I stay firmly in place, watching this other person talk to Audrey and calm her down. She's clearly freaking out about jumping.

Cline crosses his arms and sighs. "This is such a shit show, Elliot. Why are you involving yourself in this?"

"Why are you running away from it? You two haven't even talked … *really* talked yet. And now you're just going to get into the car with someone else and give up? Go back?"

"She's got problems, man. You can't fix them. I can't fix them. We don't even know what they are. But look at her. She can't even do the thing she came to do. This is nothing but a waste of time and …"

Silence follows as we both watch in awe as September leads Audrey to the edge of the cliff and holds her hand. She looks her in the eye, giving Audrey her undivided attention, and Audrey nods as if agreeing while looking down into the water thirty feet below. It's a huge drop, and I don't blame her one bit for the apprehension. September points to the water and then presses a finger to Audrey's forehead. I wish I could hear what's being said, but of all the things we've done on this trip, this seems like the most private thing I've been witness to.

September takes a step back, and I watch with my hands balled into fists as Audrey steps all the way to the edge of rock and extends her arms to her sides. She looks up to the sky once and then, for a split second before she moves, she looks over her shoulder to where we are standing, and I swear I can see her smile. The next instant, she is airborne, free falling headfirst into the water below, slicing the surface and going under, leaving nothing but a white ring of water in her wake.

There's a scream of excitement from September and then from Audrey as she resurfaces, taking in air and shrieking that she did it. Her arms are raised above her head, and she's telling all of us to come on, asking us what we're waiting for.

Cline turns to look at me, his face pale and eyes wide with shock. "What the hell did I just see?"

I clap a hand on his shoulder as I go to pass him. "You just saw Byrdie fly."

Audrey

I feel invincible. I am invincible. That's a terrifying way for someone to feel when they've felt like nothing for so long.

September is smiling at me from across the table in the little restaurant where we've decided to get lunch. The guys are playing video games in the back room of the pizza joint while we wait on our order, and I'm sipping some water, just trying to get hold of the rush of emotions I've been through in such a short amount of time.

"When were you diagnosed?" she asks. There's no malice or judgment in her question.

I look around to make sure Elliot and Cline aren't within earshot before I answer. "Fifteen. Some stuff feels like it's gotten better, but recently …"

"Obviously I'm not trying to give you any advice or treatment. I'm not a doctor. Yet." She smiles, and it's so genuine. "Are you seeing someone, though?"

"Yeah." The condensation on my glass has suddenly become very interesting.

"I know we've just met and whatever, but if you feel like you ever need to talk about stuff, and you can't with either of those two," she points to the game room, "I'm more than happy to be a listening ear. What you did today was huge. I don't even know your deal, and I can tell that it was a giant step for whatever it is that you're going through. And you should be proud of that."

"Well, maybe one day I'll tell you why it was such a big deal. Because you're right. It was. It *is* a huge deal. We only have a couple more places to go before this trip is over, and once we're done, I don't think Cline will ever speak to me again. And if Elliot finds out the truth about me ... about everything ... I have no idea if he'll stick around either. So you may just be the only one left to call." The idea strikes me suddenly even as I say it out loud. This is why I don't get involved with anyone. This is why I don't open up to people. It's all on the surface so no one gets hurt. Especially me. But I chose Elliot. I sought him out. I still can't figure out why.

Her head is tilted in thought. "I don't think there's anything short of telling Elliot that you're a murderer that would make him walk away from you. Even then, I'd bet he would try to find evidence against it. Have you seen the way he looks at you?"

"No," I lie and cross my legs as the memory of his touch from earlier in the day resurfaces.

"Then maybe you should open your eyes a little more," she says quietly and takes a sip of her drink before the pizza we ordered is placed on the table.

Elliot is sitting in the back of the car again, laptop plugged in as he tries to work on his game. A familiar tug of responsibility settles in my gut, and I chastise myself for possibly costing him this opportunity.

"Is there anything I can do to help you with this?" I ask, peering around to look at his screen.

A webpage disappears, and his work comes back up quickly with a click of his fingers. He blinks a few times and smiles at me with a shake of his head. "I'm good. It's boring."

"What were you looking at?" I ask, climbing into the back of the car next to him.

"Stuff for the project. How To's and things like that. I don't have my degree yet, you know. I'm still a novice."

"A How To on what?" I don't think Elliot's lied to me before, and now I know he's very bad at it.

"How to …" he stalls, and I can almost see his brain firing all cylinders to try and come up with something, "make realistic sand."

"Bullshit. I've seen your realistic sand. What were you looking at? Is it porn or something? Let me see!" I'm practically crawling over him to get to the laptop and switch screens so I can see what he's trying so desperately to hide from me.

"Seriously, it's nothing! Come on, Audrey, don't mess with the laptop …"

He doesn't fight hard, though, and I'm too fast. In an instant I wish I hadn't asked.

SIX TYPES OF ANXIETY ATTACKS

My eyes scan the article and I can feel my throat tightening.

Rage and irritability

Obsessive behavior

Stuttering

Silence

Zoning out

Hyperventilating/rocking back and forth

The pressure on my chest is growing heavier with each second, and I'm trying to fight it off, but I know when it's too late. This is one of those times.

"You could have asked," I whisper before I scramble to get out of the car and walk as fast as I can to the tent. I know exactly where I'm going and what I'm getting, and as soon as I have it, I am back out and into the night, walking off into the woods. I need a tree. I need a safe space. A place away from anyone and everyone else where it can happen, and I can let it overtake me until it's over and then I can move on.

The Klonopin won't kick in immediately, but at least I have that hope to hold onto as I stumble into the woods and away from the voices of the people I know. I'm walking blindly into the darkness, trying to get away from any and all light that isn't the moon, so I can't be seen. The only sounds around me are the cicadas, the water from the lake to my left, and my own erratic breathing.

It's getting harder to see, because the tears are building and blinding me, and my throat is so constricted I can hardly get a full breath in through my mouth. But if I try to breathe through my nose, I feel like I'm choking. There's a huge tree right in front of me, and I lean against it, my arms straight and legs extended, face pointed down at the ground as I try to breathe just one full breath.

But it's not coming.

The sounds coming out of my mouth would make any passerby believe I was having an asthma attack and needing an inhaler. The shaking in my hands and arms give way to numbness in my digits, and my face begins to tingle, lips losing feeling while I gasp for a single lungful of oxygen.

The world is collapsing around me, and I am alive and awake to see it all happening, but there's nothing I can do about it. Tears flow faster, and my heart beats wildly until I slide to my knees and press my face between them and begin to count silently, hoping that maybe by the time I reach ten I'll have some control.

I reach three hundred and feel a warm hand on my back. I reach three hundred and fifty when I hear September's voice. I reach four hundred when Cline picks me up and carries me back to the tent.

I lose count when Elliot wraps his body around mine in the sleeping bag and whispers that he's sorry while pushing my sweaty hair from my forehead.

His touch is what allows that first real burst of air into my lungs, and I pull it in with such force I almost choke on it, wheezing and gasping as I inhale and cry through the exhale. But he holds me through it until the pain in my chest begins to loosen. Until the tightness in my throat lessens, and I can swallow and speak. Until the vice around my head unclenches and the fuzzy gray patterns behind my eyelids give way to actual shapes again.

The campsite is quiet by the time my mind and body go into rest, and I hold Elliot's hand to my chest as I fall into a dreamless sleep.

Their voices are hushed, but I can hear them as they discuss me by the small fire they started after I fell asleep. Sometime in the night, they got up to talk, leaving me by myself, probably thinking the episode would have knocked me out. But I didn't take my nightly pills, so the insomnia caused by the morning ones has caused me to wake up suddenly, very alert.

"She had a really big day. The jump and every-thing." September's voice is quiet.

"Don't forget riding Elliot's dick earlier." Cline's voice is not quiet at all.

"I'm not going to tell you again that we didn't

have sex. We didn't. Not that it should matter to you or that it's any of your business, but we didn't. And even if we did, that wouldn't be part of this equation in any way." My heart skips at the sound of Elliot's voice and the thought that he feels like being with me might have had something to do with this.

"It could be any number of things or it could be nothing at all. These things aren't by the book. Panic attacks, anxiety attacks—they happen for a lot of reasons, and they happen in a lot of ways. But if you guys are going to be traveling with her for the next week or so, you're going to have to know how to handle it if she has another one," September outlines for them.

"That's what I was trying to look up when she saw my laptop. That's why she freaked out." Elliot's explanation is making my heart race again.

"You should come with us. Just in case." Cline is asking September to stay for his own reasoning but using me as justification. I should be pissed, but I'm not. I like her. And I like him when he's with her.

"I'll think about it. You only have a couple more stops before you go back to Tennessee, right? If that's the case, I can put off going back home for a little while longer."

The chatter begins to die down, and I hear them say goodnight. The zipper opens, and Elliot steps back inside as quietly as he possibly can. He slips back into the makeshift bed with me and pulls my back to his chest, securing me to him with his arm over my stomach.

I listen to him sleep for the next six hours until the sun comes up and I have an excuse to get up and go take a shower. My reflection mocks me with puffy eyes and tangled hair. This nagging voice in my head that sounds irritatingly a lot like Miranda expresses to me me that I'm not good enough anyway, and I should just let Elliot go. I'm tainted and wrong and broken, and he can't fix me. This trip is a waste. I'm hopeless.

And for the first time in a very long time, I nod

in the mirror and think that maybe I am a lost cause. Maybe I finally agree.

I just won't let any of them know yet.

I've had my shower, taken my pills, and had a cup of coffee. All of those earlier thoughts are scattered, and I am focused on cooking our last breakfast at the campsite. Bacon and eggs on Elliot's dad's old skillet, plus biscuits from a bag. I'm not a gourmet cook, but I can work with what I've got.

I'm slicing some apples when Cline emerges from September's tent.

"Whoa, you want some help with that?" He asks, hands raised and eyebrows drawn in concern.

I frown. "Are you afraid of me having a knife? Really, Cline? It was a panic attack. I should shank you just for being a dickhead."

He nods and shrugs a shoulder. "So, you're okay, then. Good to see you're back to normal,

Byrdie."

I don't even flinch at his use of my old nick-name. I just hand him a cup of coffee and point to the bacon. "Save some for Elliot. That man loves his bacon."

"Since when is Elliot a man?" Cline asks as he shoves a piece of pork in his mouth.

"Since he made me come in under a minute."

"Damnit, Audrey, I'm trying to eat!" Cline slaps the picnic table and shoots me a disgusted look.

"What's going on?" Elliot steps out of the tent, his dark hair standing up in all directions, his eyes still half closed with sleep.

"I was telling Cline about your super powers, and he's all jealous and stuff."

"Shut *up*, woman!" Cline makes a move like he's going to get up.

"Able to hit a g-spot in three-point-five sec-onds!" I yell, just to piss him off. I'm successful, and he takes his plate of bacon, stomping off back into the other tent. I smile at Elliot and offer him a plate. "Hungry?"

He takes it and sits down across from me, eyeing me warily. "Are you okay?"

"Yeah, I feel great. Sorry about yesterday. I think it was just a lot of excitement and emotions. Everything should be okay from now on. I promise." Lying to people about being fine has become such second nature that I don't even know I'm doing it most of the time. I do right now, though. Elliot doesn't deserve to be lied to. I just can't shake the voices in my head from earlier and the thoughts they planted there, even if they're quieter now than before.

"If it was my fault …"

"No. None of it was. You're great. You've been great and you're amazing. We're going to Alabama next. Then Mississippi. Then back to Tennessee. After that, you've got the rest of your summer to do whatever with. And hopefully you'll have everything you need to make a kick ass game and become a billionaire. I'll get a magazine with your face on it and tell my friends you had your hand down my pants once. It'll be my claim to fame."

"Audrey …" His lips are pulled thin.

"What?" I laugh and stand up again, stepping away from the table. "Besides some merchandise with my cookie shitting unicorn—"

"Stop." He gets up, too, and comes around the table to stand toe to toe with me. With a gentle tug, he pulls me with him back inside the tent. It's starting to feel like home, and that's exactly why we need to take it down immediately and get back in the car to our next destination. "When this trip is over, I don't plan on just walking away from this. Whatever this is."

"This?" I ask. "We made out. It got weird. We slept in a sleeping bag together a few times. We can go back to being friends and stuff."

"I don't want to, though." His hands are on my hips, and I can't even look him in the eye.

"But I do."

"You're a terribly bad liar. Is this because of last night? I can handle last night. If you'll just talk to me about what's going on with you—all of what's going on with you, then—"

"I don't even know what's going on with me, Elliot. Okay? That's the truth. All this shit up here? I don't know where it comes from. I don't know the source, so I don't know how to fix it. If I can't fix it, you can't fix it. So all I'm going to do it mess up your life and everyone else's life just like I did for my mom and Patrick and Miranda. Granny Ruth. And this other guy? Who is he? Who the hell knows what happened to him. I'm a human stain. Cline's right. You should run as far away as you can, because I'm just gonna fuck everything up for you."

"Holy shit. That's what you think? You think because you get sad sometimes or you do weird things to cope with feeling overwhelmed, or you have panic attacks, that you ruin people's lives?"

I'm silent, because I know the answer and he does, too. I expect that this is the moment he grabs his stuff and walks away. Or tells me to get another ride home. Instead, he laughs.

"This is really going to suck for you."

"What is?" I ask.

He leans in close so that his lips are right next to my ear, and he whispers, sending goosebumps down my neck and arm, "You're going to find out that I'm not going to give up on you over something as stupid as that. Then you're going to realize you're worth fighting for. And I'm going to be the one to prove it to you."

Audrey

Jumping from the cliff takes my breath away, a rush of excitement flowing through my arms, up around my sternum into my chest cavity where I can feel my heart almost explode out of my chest. The water is chilly as I land and slice through, arms extended, breath held, eyes open. Everything is green and white, bubbles from my lips and nose rising to surface as I begin to exhale.

My mother is staring back at me from beneath the water, smiling, her hair long and swirling around us both.

It shocks me and I inhale, suddenly aware that I should be choking, but I'm not. I can breathe. I can breathe underwater?

I try again, and once more, I am breathing but still submerged. She's still there, treading along with me, smiling with encouragement, and I reach out to touch her, but my hands are balled into fists. I can't unclench them, and I watch, panic stricken, as I begin to sink, unable to extend a hand to ask for help, but I am still breathing, watching her disappear as I sink deeper into the darkness.

"Audrey, we're making a stop." Elliot's voice pulls me from my dream, and I wake with a start in the front seat of his car, covered in summer afternoon sweat. My feet are bare against his dashboard, and there's a kink in my neck that reminds me that I am very much alive and most likely not a mermaid that can breathe underwater. This is both a good revelation and something that makes me sad at the same time.

I've never dreamt of my mom before, and it's left me a little shaken.

The gas station isn't very busy, and after I've gone to the restroom, I spend a few minutes walking the aisles to see if there's anything I'd like to eat. Maybe a treat I'd like to get for Elliot to say thank you for just ... being himself. There's a large display of mega-sized Rice Krispy Treats on an end cap, and I grab one, bringing the wrapper to my nose and inhaling to see if I can smell it.

It's faint, but the aroma is there, and for a moment, my heart clenches as memories of Patrick bringing plates of them to our little hideout in the backyard come rushing back. Cline could never have just one. He always had one in each hand like his mom could catch him at any moment and he'd have to shove them both in his mouth in a desperate attempt to have one last sweet before going back to the land of juicing and dehydrated fruits.

I don't even hear him approach. I can feel him standing behind me before I open my eyes to acknowledge that he's there. "Do you remember the last time we had these?" I ask.

Cline reaches over my shoulder and takes one of the packages in his hand, turning the bright blue wrapper around. "Probably when we were twelve. My mom found out your dad had given them to me because they were stuck in my hair."

I turn and regard him with a laugh. "Were you trying to save some for a snack later?"

The look in his eyes is anything but amused. He's sizing me up like he's deciding whether or not to ask a question. I'm hyper aware of everything in that space in time. The smell of the store. The crinkle of the wrapper in my hand. The buzzing of the fluorescent lights. How unfocused my eyesight is as I become lightheaded waiting for him to speak.

He clears his throat and looks down at his hands and then back up at me, a tick in his jaw alerting me to the seriousness of the situation. "Did you run away because of me? Was it my fault, Byrdie?"

Every last thing that I've ever wanted to say to him builds up inside of my throat, and the pressure in my chest expands until I'm sure I'm going to pass out. This isn't the time and place for it, though. I have a plan, and it does not involve standing in front of the beer refrigerator of a Chevron gas station. I wait a few seconds and gather my thoughts before I speak, even though I can sense that my silence is giving Cline more of an answer than a simple yes or no would.

"I didn't run away. So, no."

He holds my gaze, our eyes locked and bodies only inches apart for what feels like the first time in eons. He's so familiar and yet the most foreign thing in my entire life right now. "Why would your dad lie about that? Tell everyone you ran away if you didn't?" He asks, his voice low and a little shaky.

I shrug and look away, grabbing another treat before I sidestep him. "Some lies are easier to say out loud than telling people the truth." There's no reason for me to turn around and look at his face as I walk away. There's confusion and hurt there that I've seen so many times before, more than I could possibly keep count of. Part of this trip is making that right, but I'm forcing myself to take my therapist's advice and stick with the plan I have in my head. Ignoring the impulse to tell him everything in the here and now is overwhelming. and that's exactly how I know it's not right.

It's not time.

The first day I met Dr. Stark. she didn't look at me with pity or like I was some kind of miracle. She didn't treat me as if I were some sort of hopeless thing that couldn't be cured. She treated me like a person, and I didn't know how to respond to that.

The first session began with the question, "What brings you here?" And I answered with a name, so she cut me off. It wasn't *who* brought me there. There was no one person that caused me to end up in her office. No two people were responsible for my time spent in the hospital while Patrick and Miranda played damage control and lied that I'd run away. I half expected to hear the therapist tell me no one can make you feel inferior without your consent, but she stopped just shy of that.

She asked for a complete history. A full rundown. So I told her everything, down to the very last moment I could remember, and she wrote her notes all the while. She would cross and uncross her legs, nod and stop writing at particular intervals if something of note would come out of my mouth. Otherwise, she was nothing but professional, and by the end of that first session, I think I had told her everything I could think of, starting from the moment I was born until that very second I was in her office.

There was blame and guilt everywhere, almost as if I could see it piling up on the ground around me. The more I spoke, the more carnage, the higher the body count, there was. Everyone had a hand in my misery and owned a bit of why I was sitting in front of this slender woman with honey colored hair and a blank expression as I bared my fifteen-year-old soul.

By the time I was done, I was a mess, both emotionally and physically. I'd cried until I was dry, and my body hurt from the act of it. But all she did was offer me a tissue and then a small piece of advice that changed the course of my life forever. "Now that you're done blaming everyone else for your troubles, we can start working on the root of the problems inside of *you*, Audrey. Let's figure out where *those* come from."

It was the inability to understand the origin of that—where those issues arose from—that had confounded me so deeply. I had no sense of who I really was or where I had truly come from. Now the only people who knew the truth were a few adults who were paid to know my secrets or were trying to pretend they didn't exist.

Then I got assigned Cara, the voice on the other end of the phone. My weekly check-in to make sure everything is still okay. A twisted kind of pen pal or internet friend, but we'd been relegated to speaking only by phone and for the express purpose of my mental wellbeing.

Sitting in the car with Elliot as we drive back into Alabama, I wonder if there will come a time where I can tell someone else how I'm feeling instead of depending on a Tuesday night call. I wonder if this plan that my therapist set in motion, where I let go of these preconceived notions about the guilt I associated with each person I blamed for having a hand in what happened all those years ago, will actually make a difference. I wonder if I'll come out on the other side like some sort of monarch butterfly. Maybe I'll end up like that confused moth in the bathroom, bumping into everything and trying to escape a bathroom stall instead.

I wonder how September will be as a psychologist when she finally establishes her own practice. When we were up on the cliff and I was melting down, she was so kind and reassuring. She knew before I even said anything. It must have been the fear in my eyes. Or the way I curled up into a ball and started freaking out about how there was no way in hell I was going over that ledge. She told me it was all in my head. Her touch was so tender and reassuring. Her voice was so calm and soothing. Her eyes held mine while we spoke and she encouraged me to face my fears.

A smile plays at my lips as a thought hits me suddenly. With the way Cline has become interested in her so quickly, would she end up practicing as September Worley? Or September Somers?

"What are you smiling about over there?" Elliot asks as he pulls up to a red light. September and Cline pull up beside us, and I look over to see the two of them talking with the windows down, huge, stupid smiles on their faces. They're so into each other it's ridiculous.

"If those two get married, then her name will forever be September Somers." I say without any sarcasm at all.

"They've known each other for all of three days. I don't think you can start planning a wedding for them yet," Elliot says as the light turns green.

We pull ahead of them at least thirty seconds before September even realizes that the signal has changed, and I turn to glance back over at the boy sitting to my left. "I have a hunch about this one. I know we're not close anymore, but he's pretty easy to read when it comes to girls. I haven't seen him this into someone before. Not even Kelsey. And I'm pretty sure his twelve-year-old brain thought he was going to marry her one day."

Elliot's shoulders raise a bit and he grips the wheel tightly, eyes still on the road. "Do you think you'll ever trust me enough to tell me what actually happened between the two of you?"

I shrug and look back out the window, unsure of my answer. "I don't know. Because the answer is that *nothing* happened between us. That's the problem." It's still unclear how I'm supposed to apologize for walking away from a friendship without any explanation, because it was best for me at the time, and best for him in the long run.

I have three days to figure out the words to say it, though.

Elliot

There's a part of me that has wanted to look at Wendy's journals when Audrey has left them unattended so that I can see what she's reading while I drive or when she's having one of her quiet moments. I know how bothered I would be if I found anyone looking through my dad's stuff though, so I don't.

The first letters he sent weren't much, just blue pages saying how much he missed my mom.

They'd always start with "Roseanna baby,"and they'd always end with "All my love, Pete." That first deployment was directly after 9/11, and his unit was one of the first ones in—mobile and unestablished—so we couldn't call. Couldn't send mail. We could only receive it. He'd send small letters for me, too, but they weren't much, just enough for me to read that he missed me.

The deployments weren't long, but they were back to back, and in a two year span he did three deployments to both Iraq and Afghanistan. My mom had been glued to the television, watching reports as hostages were rescued and bombs were detonated. Each time the doorbell rang, she would go pale, and now I know what she was waiting for, but at the time, it was usually just my friends coming over to play. I didn't understand her anxiousness until I got much older.

He was on his final deployment when it happened. A car bomb at a check point. You're not allowed a lot of information, and they keep secrets about plenty of things that happen overseas, but the way my father died was heroic, and they were sure to tell me that at his funeral. That he'd died running toward the other men in his unit, trying to save their lives. His name lives on, printed on silver bracelets that his friends wear in his memory, along with the five other men that died that day.

He left behind a grieving wife, a confused eight-year-old son, a box of letters, and a photo album full of pictures of him in Afghanistan with people he considered his brothers. Face covered in dirt and sun beating down on everything. He was proud. He was doing something.

Part of me hopes that by doing this thing for Audrey, that maybe I'm doing something, too. Something my dad would be proud of. He'd always been so supportive of my interests and how my brain functioned, my love of building and how I wanted to know exactly how everything worked. I'd spend hours building Legos and wait until I could barely keep my eyes open just to hear him come through the door and tell me that I was the best builder he'd ever seen.

My game is not in memoriam. It's in his honor.

Sitting at the small desk in a cheap hotel just outside of Mobile, Alabama, I remind myself of that as I put the final touches on a character that looks exactly like my father. His eyes stare back at me from the screen, eerily lifelike. I don't know whether to laugh or shut my laptop and take a walk around the pool to clear my head.

Audrey appears at that exact moment, opening the bathroom door, wearing a red sundress. The straps are thin, pulled up and across her back in an interesting pattern that catches my attention when she turns around to check her reflection in the full length mirror. She'd asked to stop at the store on our way into town, and I'd seen her grab the dress along with a few other items, almost like she didn't want to get it but couldn't stop herself from buying it.

"I didn't know if it would fit my boobs," she

says out loud and then turns to me with wide eyes. "Probably not something you're used to hearing. Sorry about that." Her cheeks almost match the color of the material she's wearing. For what it's worth, it does fit her boobs. Very well, if I'm being honest. Maybe a little too well, according to how fast I have to look away.

"You look pretty," I say as I save my work and close my laptop. She's still and staring at me as I turn around to face her again. "What? You do. It's a good color on you. I like the hair, too." She bought a box of dye and went one color, a dark brown, almost black, all over, covering the lighter ends. It makes her eyes stand out more.

"Please stop saying nice things to me. I don't know how to take compliments. They make me feel awkward," she says and begins to pull at the dress.

I stand and walk over to her, taking her hands in mine. "You just say thank you and move on. Try it."

Her chest blossoms bright pink, and she

breathes heavily as we hold eye contact. I swear I can see tears begin to form in her eyes before she looks away. "Thank you." Stepping back, she pulls her hands from mine and reaches into the plastic bag on her bed, pulling out two hats. "I bought one of each. Wasn't sure who you wanted to represent in this neck of the woods. We are a house divided today, Mr. Clark. Are you going to yell Roll Tide?" She extends the burgundy hat my way then scrunches her face up and shakes her head. "Do that thing where you make the bill less flat. That thing boys do. It's a magic power I don't possess." She stands there, staring at the hat with a dubious look on her face then flops it in my direction with a silent demand for me to fix it.

I laugh while I bend the brim and wait for her to get the rest of her stuff together before we leave. From the corner of my eye I can see her rummaging around for another couple of orange bottles, and then she takes a quick swig of water before turning to me like nothing has just happened.

"The Lovebirds should be waiting for us downstairs. Are you ready to experience deep fried butter?" She asks, holding her hand out for mine.

"I'm going to pass on that," I say, holding the hotel room door open for her and allowing her to pass through before me. "I want to live past the age of twenty-two. Death by calories wouldn't be my suicide of choice."

Her hand is gone from mine in an instant, suddenly fidgeting with a pin in her hair. "Sorry," she mumbles. "It was falling." But she doesn't give me her hand back on the elevator ride down.

Cline and September are waiting for us by the doors, and Audrey has a smile plastered on her face by the time we reach the both of them. She extends her hand in offering, giving Cline the Auburn Tigers hat as a gift. He appears surprised for all of two seconds before finding his composure and taking it from her. The bill is broken in by the time we've made it to the fairgrounds, and the awkward moment in the hotel hallway is long forgotten under the sounds of kids screaming and yelling on rides. The smell of fried food hangs heavy in the air, and my stomach rumbles with want.

The sky has been light gray all day, but as night begins to fall, the clouds are drawing closer and deepening to a darker hue. The air feels thick with humidity, and my arms are coated with wetness within a few minutes of being out of the air conditioning of my car.

September has her hair pulled up into a bun, pieces escaping around her face and sticking to her forehead as she stares up at the giant Ferris wheel while Cline and I buy ride tickets. Her dress is strapless, and she's wearing boots, effortlessly pretty and comfortable in her own skin next to Audrey who is twisting her hair into a knot and letting it go, over and over again. The difference between the two of them as they stand side by side is glaringly obvious.

I come to stand behind Audrey and lean into her ear. "Want me to put your hair up for you?"

Even in the warmth of an Alabama summer, the feel of my breath on her neck causes goosebumps to arise, and instead of answering me, she pulls a ponytail holder from around her wrist and offers it to me. Her attention goes to the aluminum bracelet around her wrist again, and I wish for once she could find some semblance of calm for longer than thirty seconds.

I secure her ponytail and turn her around to face me with a smile and a nod. "Perfect. Are we going on the Ferris wheel?"

"Not a chance in hell, Elliot. But I'll let you take me on that zero gravity ride over there." She points to a circular ride where people are standing, but the machine is moving so fast they're forced against the sliding wall, paralyzed. Every single rider is screaming their heads off and laughing all at once.

"I'm in," comes September's reply, and she takes a handful of tickets from Cline in one hand and Audrey's palm in the other. The two girls take off, and I'm left with Cline, watching them go.

"She blew me in the shower," he blurts out.

"What the hell, man? I don't need to know that." I throw a disgusted look his way and start walking after the girls.

He jogs a second to catch up, his eyes wide. "You might. See how close they are? My girl could be, like, *hey Audrey, want to share a soda*? And she'd be all, like, *oh, yeah, let's do that, but only one straw because we're girls and we do weird shit like that*. And then you'll be kissing Audrey later tonight and—"

I punch him right in the arm to get him to shut up.

"Ow!" he yells.

A man walking by with an Alabama hat on just like mine tips it at me and crows, "That's right! Roll Tide!"

"You're wearing the wrong hat tonight," I say and punch Cline again. He flinches and pretends like he's going to punch me back but doesn't follow through. Instead, he pulls me under his arm and steals my hat, running off with it over his head as he meets up with the girls waiting by the ride.

It's started to sprinkle, and we've ridden five rides so far, walked the entire length of the fairgrounds, and watched a group of nine year olds tap dance in skirts bigger than my bedroom. The smile on Audrey's face is enormous, and I can't stop staring at her.

She's holding a funnel cake in one hand and a custard in the other while I balance a corn dog and massive soda myself. Cline and September have gotten on the Ferris wheel, and it will be at least another ten minutes before they make it to the top and all the way back around. We head away from the lights and sounds toward the grass and rocks of a field just beyond the parameters of the fairgrounds. There's a slight breeze as we go to sit, and Audrey's skirt flies up, making her laugh and attempt to grab it with both of her full hands. She's unsuccessful and ends up landing on her ass gracelessly, powdered sugar sliding from the plate onto her lap in the process.

"Figures. I'm over here trying to act like a lady, and all the elements are against me." She shakes her fist at the sky in false anger.

"You don't have to act like a lady," I tell her just as I turn to look and see that she's taken a huge bite out of the funnel cake and has white powder all over her cheeks and under her nose. "I retract that statement. Maybe trying a *little* bit would be helpful."

Her laugh causes more powdered sugar to go flying into the air. She passes the food over to me, and we share it until it's all gone and we've cleaned up the best we can, though her red dress has spots that won't come out without a good washing. The sprinkles of water are doing little to help with the situation. They simply disappear into the fabric as soon as they make contact.

We stare at the lights of the fair beyond us, such a stark contrast to the dark night sky, obliterating any stars that are shining above it. It reminds me of how I feel when I'm around Audrey. How loud and bright and chaotic she can be. How she can swallow the entire environment around her until she's the only focal point. She could dim even the brightest of stars if she'd just get out of her head.

My attention is back on her as my thoughts turn in my head and I can see her staring back up at me, the flashing lights in the distance reflected in her dark eyes. I lean forward and she doesn't move, just keeps watching as I advance.

"You want me to kiss you so badly right now," I say.

Her eyebrows draw together and she snorts, her eyes darting away instead of holding steady with my own. "No, I don't."

"Yes, you do. I can see it. But, I'm not going to. Not until you ask me. Because I think that's a thing for you—asking people to do stuff. Asking for things. So, when you finally decide you're ready for that kiss, you just let me know."

She leans back on her elbows and looks up at the sky, her ponytail dragging along the grass as her eyes close and the rain hits her face lightly. "Nah. You'll be waiting forever and a day, Elliot. I'm not gonna ask you to kiss me. We should keep it just like this. All this yearning. This build up to nothing. Will they? Won't they?" Her eyes open and she looks over her shoulder at me, teasing, but her face is serious. "We're gonna be the greatest love story never told."

Audrey

Somewhere along this trip I was supposed to find my mother. Some shred of closeness to her or a glimpse of who she was that would help me feel bonded to her in some way. But I feel more detached as the days wear on. I don't feel like I'm learning more about Wendy.

Maybe I'm figuring myself out instead.

There's a heaviness that's settling on my shoulders as we travel into Mississippi, because it's our final stop and the one that I've been both looking forward to and dreading the most. First, this is September's home state, so once we're done here, she's staying, and I have no idea how this will impact Cline. Second, this is the place where I tell him everything, and afterward, I think maybe he'll want to stay with her, and I might be a complete mess. The weight of what is to come gnaws at my insides and makes my stomach hurt, causes my head to feel heavy, the medications running through my veins protesting against the impending drop in serotonin.

My instinct is to curl into a ball and sleep. Maybe this was a bad idea. Perhaps everything I think will turn out okay is actually going to blow up in my face, and it will end a thousand times worse than anything I could even imagine. With shaking fingers, I reach beneath my seat and blindly grab for my bag. I've become so used to having it there in my time of need that it's second nature to pull it out now. There was a time where I thought maybe feeling too much was better than not feeling anything at all, but I learned quickly that I was very, very wrong.

Elliot's voice breaks through the chatter in my mind that sounds so loud it's as if I've been having a full conversation out loud in the cab of the car by myself. And yet, we've been driving in silence, just the sound of the radio playing on low as background noise. "We're going to grab some lunch at this place right up here. Are you hungry?"

The concern in his eyes jumpstarts my heart just the tiniest bit, working its way beneath the fog building around my brain. I place a smile on my face, as usual, and nod. "I'm starving." I want bread. Carbs. Sugar. I'm suddenly craving anything I can get my hands on which might make me feel a little bit better about myself. Miranda would call this "eating my feelings."

Cline and September are waiting in the parking lot, leaning against the back of her car, sucking face as we approach.

"Get a room," Elliot jokes, poking Cline in the

neck, knowing damn good and well that's his most ticklish spot.

The Giant giggles like a girl and folds in half, then stands and straightens like he's a man and narrows his eyes at his roommate. "We had a deal, man. That was a secret to the grave."

Elliot shrugs. "I didn't *tell* anyone you were ticklish. Technically, I just showed them. It's more of a loophole than anything."

They're still arguing over semantics as we're being seated and handed our menus. I'm sitting across from September, who is clearly enjoying the majestic display of manly ego. Her halter top is a bright orange and brown Aztec print, and she's wearing turquoise jewelry that offsets her tan and dark coloring. I can't stop staring at how incredibly pretty she is and marveling at how inferior I feel in her presence, yet how much she makes me feel at ease.

Her green eyes meet mine across the table and she grins, all white teeth and freckles. "You doing okay?"

"Yeah, I'm fine. Why? Do I look like I'm not fine? Because, I am." My fingers are tearing at the edge of the menu, and I can't get situated in the booth's seat comfortably to save my life.

Her face turns serious, and she reaches out like she's going to comfort me, but I retract my hands from her reach. I don't need attention drawn to what's going on right now.

"Are you upset about something? Do you need to talk?" she's asking, and the fact that she looks like she cares, and her voice sounds like it, too, is making tears start to form in my eyes, and I blink furiously to keep them at bay.

"I said I'm fine. Really. I just want to get something to eat. And I don't exactly know where this tree is that we're supposed to go to tonight, so that's stressing me out a little bit. Then, you know, this is your last day with us … but otherwise, I'm fine." I haven't noticed that the entire table has gone silent and all eyes are on me. Somehow during my speech, I've decimated two napkins and they are laying in a torn-up pile in front of me.

"You seem like you're handling things like a champ," Cline says lowly, eyeing the wreckage on the table.

"You think this is stressed?" I ask. "Did you know that an octopus will eat itself when it gets stressed out? *That's* not handling things well. *That's* overdramatic. I'd say I'm doing just fine." I nod my head, eyes wide, trying to convince them of my sanity but fear that I'm failing miserably.

Cline narrows his eyes. "Given the fact that there are certain species of male octopus that detach their own dick and throw it at a female so she can get herself pregnant and then grow a new dick afterwards, I don't think *that's* the animal I'd be comparing myself to if I wanted to maintain any level of normalcy."

Elliot's laugh cuts through the tension, causing me to flinch. "Wait … The octopus just throws it at her? Like, javelins it through the water?"

Now September is laughing, too, making a motion with her arm like she's throwing a dick. "Here, take it, you hot piece of eight-armed ass! You've earned it. I'll just grow another one, see?"

Cline leans in close to the side of her face and kisses next to her ear. "You're so hot. Do you really have to stay here? Can't you come back with me for the rest of the summer?"

When she turns her head, they are only an inch apart, and I can't tear my eyes away from them.

"We're only one state away. I have stuff I have to do here. I'll visit before I go back to school, I promise," she says quietly.

"I'll go wherever you want me to," he whispers back.

"Oh, gross. Stop. You sound like those crappy love songs on the radio, and you're making me want to throw up." I hold my menu up to my face to block them out.

"What do have against love songs on the radio?" Elliot asks to my right as he looks over his menu, not making eye contact.

"Don't tell me you believe in that stuff. Come on. All of that 'if the world came crashing down, I would be holding you, watching the sky fall on us, waiting for the earth to explode …' That's not even feasible. And let me tell you something, okay? If the world was spinning into another planet and the sky was falling or the core of the earth was about to explode, I'd be running. And you'd better be running, too." I chance a glance over at Elliot, and he's grinning down at the menu. "What?" I ask, lowering mine to my lap.

"I mean, I get what you're saying. I don't really believe in love songs, either. And that was a great speech you just made. But I think you might change your mind one day."

"And why is that?" I ask, my heart anxiously skipping a beat in my chest.

His grin grows wider, but he still doesn't look my way. "Because you said I should be running, too. I was part of the 'we' in that scenario you just made up."

September's house is bigger than expected, and her family is nowhere to be found.

"They're on vacation until next week, so we have the place to ourselves. You're all welcome to stay as long as you want to. You don't have to leave unless you really need to go. I have enough room for all of you." She walks us through the large foyer and shows us around the downstairs, pointing out the fully stocked, spotless kitchen. The living room has a seventy inch television hung above a fake fireplace, and her backyard has a full-sized pool, complete with a diving board. Upstairs are five bedrooms, and she immediately invites Cline to stay with her, which he does not object to at all. She offers the guest bedroom to Elliot and myself, but also points out that I'm more than welcome to stay in Thursday's room if I prefer.

Elliot's face is completely smooth and expressionless when I place my bag in the guest bedroom with his.

"The tree is about twenty five miles from here, so we should get changed and head out around nine, according to what my mom wrote about the place," I tell him as I start pulling things out of my overnight bag.

"What exactly is this again?" Elliot asks, sitting heavily on the queen size bed and falling backward onto it, his head rolled to the side so he can face me as I continue to pull out clothes for the night.

"It's called The Confession Tree. It's in the woods off the side of these intersecting neighborhoods, behind a cemetery. The tree itself is dead, and the top is rotted off, but the base is really tall. It's hollow and someone carved out a hole, like a doorway, where people can get inside. Wendy's journal said that she went there with a group of people she was traveling with right before she met Patrick, and they took turns going in two at a time and confessing things to one another. I don't know exactly what." I gather up my toiletries and turn to face his curious gaze.

"You already know what you're going to say, don't you." It's not a question. Elliot is too smart for that.

"I have things I need to tell him, Elliot. And this might be the only way I can get him to listen to me and not judge me or yell or run away. It's worth a shot. And if it backfires, then at least I'll have tried." My hands are shaking, and I hold everything closer to my body to stop it.

He sits up and looks me over, his dark eyes searching. "And me? Am I coming in with you?"

I smile. "Depends on if you have something to tell me, I guess." I don't wait for his answer before I leave the room to take a shower and prepare myself for what's coming next.

Anderson's truck is made for the type of trip we're about to embark on, and September assures us that he wouldn't have an issue with us taking it. Cline is giddy with excitement, climbing behind the driver's seat of the Chevy extended cab, adjusting the mirrors, sliding his girl closer to his side before roaring out of her driveway and into the warm Mississippi night.

We ride with the windows rolled down, a faint knowledge of where our destination should be, and nothing but headlights in front of us and the radio turned up to almost deafening levels. Cline has his head out the window, hair blowing in the wind, shouting into the night like he's lost his damn mind. Then I realize he's just happy. I've forgotten how that looks on him; it's been so long.

My hand instinctively grabs for Elliot's across the seat, and he takes it, twining our fingers together and placing our hands on his left thigh. He shifts closer, only an inch or so, but it's enough to make the tension in my shoulders relax. I chance a look at his profile in the darkness of the backseat, and he has his eyes closed while the air from the windows hits his face, the wind ruffling his dark hair back and making his eyelashes flutter in the breeze. I have fought the growing attraction inside me with every ounce of willpower that I have, but in this exact moment, I know I can't anymore.

I have feelings for him, and I am scared shitless by what that means.

After a few more minutes of staring, his eyes open, and I look away, out my window, trying to tuck my hair behind my ear like I've been enjoying the scenery outside instead of inside the cab of the truck. A pulse of his hand against mine alerts me to the twitching in my fingers, and I take a deep breath and turn to look at him again. He licks his lips and leans forward, but this time I don't back away or stay still, I move toward him, too. His cheek grazes mine and he places a soft kiss by my ear.

"We're almost there," he says, low and deep, causing me to shiver. I nod in response, and he pulls back to give me a smile of encouragement. I focus on his words and his mouth. How he says his s's. The way they come out different and thicker than anything else he says. I think about his eyes and how kind they are or how concerned he can be. What they looked like when he jumped from the cliff and came up out of the water, his head emerging and eyes seeking me out to grab me and hug me to him while he yelled in excitement.

I think about his promise and hope that after tonight he still feels the same way.

Cline slows the truck down to a crawl, and September turns from the front seat to look back at me, her gaze darting to my hand in Elliot's for only the smallest of seconds before she speaks. "Do we park here? When I looked it up, all of the sites I saw said that if the people in the neighborhood catch you they'll call the cops."

I look around at our surroundings and point beyond a stop sign. "Park in that church lot. Seems like a good place to be if we're going to be trespassing in a cemetery, right?"

Cline mumbles something, pulls in, and then puts the truck into park and waits. I look at the map I found and take a deep breath before letting go of Elliot's hand and getting out. Illuminated by only a street light, the map is lightly drawn, and I have to squint to see which direction it's pointing us to. With one flick of my wrist, I have the streets aligned and every nerve in my body is on high alert.

"It's this way," I say, turning to the group as they stand behind, waiting for instructions. "I'm ready whenever you are."

Audrey

The night is eerily quiet as we walk the length of the darkened streets of the neighborhood from one stop sign to the next. The sound of our footsteps is near deafening, and I almost want to tell everyone to tiptoe just in case anyone is out on their porch this late at night with a shotgun. I'm not a runner, but I will run from guns, ghosts, and zombies.

"Is it this fork … or this one?" Cline asks, holding up the map and shining his phone light on it.

There are two splits off of the main neighborhood road, and the map doesn't exactly differentiate between the two.

September speaks up, pointing her finger to the left. "I'm going to assume it's the split with all the scary fog and no light coming from it and not the one where you can see houses and stuff."

"Shit. She's probably right." Cline huffs and pulls her to his side. "I cannot *believe* none of us brought a gun. Or a knife. Or nunchucks."

"What would you have done with nunchucks?" Elliot hisses at him in the darkness.

"*Hit them in the balls*," Cline loud-whispers back.

We are almost to the location now, and just as we near the end of the road, a chain link fence comes into view.

"Damn. There's a fence. Guess we have to turn around and leave now—" Cline begins to turn just as Elliot lifts his phone again, using it as a flashlight straight ahead. Like some sort of sick joke, there is a massive hole cut right in the middle of the links. Fog is still rolling out of it, and right as I step off of the asphalt onto the grass in front of the opening, the temperature drops a few degrees.

"Nope. Not worth it. This is some voodoo shit right here, Byrdie. Is that really a cemetery we're supposed to cross?" Cline's eyes are silver reflections of the moon as I step through into the cemetery.

"We have to cross a bridge, too," I call over my shoulder.

"Fuck. No." I can hear him saying it, but he's right behind me, following and pulling September along with him. She's whispering something to herself, and after a second, Elliot is directly by my side.

"What is she saying?" I ask him when he gets close enough.

"She's reciting The Lord's Prayer," he answers back before he stumbles a bit and stops cold. "I'm sorry. That was a grave. I stepped on a grave. Fix it." His eyes are huge.

I push the little cement piece back into place and do a curtsy. "Our apologies."

"That's not how this works!" Cline is freaking out behind us, and suddenly I feel his hand on my shoulder, pushing me forward as he pulls September along, and Elliot is running alongside all of us. There's a sound in the trees to our right, and he quickens his pace before moving his girl next to me and shoving us both in front. With one final nudge, we're in the trees, and Cline is fumbling for a flashlight on Anderson's keychain.

"We have *got* to come prepared next time," he says through gasps of breath. The light from the tiny flashlight hits the small curved bridge that my mom had written about, and he mutters for us to keep moving, so we do. Within minutes, the trees suddenly grow sparse, and the night sky appears once more, the moon in full view above our heads.

There, right in front of us, surrounded by nothing but tall, thick grass, is the biggest tree I have ever seen in my entire life. At least, what's left of it. The roots are enormous, exposed and expanding fifteen feet or more in each direction. It's just as my mom had described it, though older and more worn. The top is gone, but still stands almost ten feet tall. The base looks like you could fit furniture inside of it and hang a television ... make it a living room. At least the kind of living rooms we're used to seeing at college.

We move around the front to the side, and there, as promised, is the carved out opening. The door to The Confession Tree.

"What time is it?" I ask, looking over to see Elliot staring down at one of the larger exposed roots.

He glances at his phone. "It's just about 10."

"Perfect. Who wants to go first?" I ask, knowing that no matter who answers, I'll have the final say. My mind is racing and every nerve is on edge. *This is it.*

"I'll go first with Cline," September offers. Her

smile is sly, and my hands begin to sweat, wondering what she has to say, but glad that he's going to have something sweet to remember about this night if I end up ruining everything.

"Cool. Head in," I say and point to the entrance. We've gone over what the tree is for. The rules have been established. Once they've disappeared, I step away so that I can't hear what's going on. I need to focus anyway. Plus, what they say is none of my business.

Elliot sounds so far away, but when I turn to find him, he's barely a foot to my right.

"What did you say?" I ask.

His eyes are gazing upward at the moon, and his jaw is set before he speaks again so I can hear. "Are we going in? The two of us, I mean. Did you decide you had something to confess to me?"

"I said we were going in if *you* had something to say to *me*."

A small smile plays along his lips and he nods. "Then I guess we're next."

If time could stand still, it does in those minutes that we are outside the tree, and yet, once the other two emerge and it's time for me to go inside with Elliot, I'm suddenly feeling like I need more of it. There's a glow about September, and Cline's smile is a mile wide, but I'm being weighted down more by the second, even as we move through the door and stand inside the dilapidated tree to face one another, toe to toe.

My heart is beating so fast, but I force myself to look up at Elliot's face as it tilts down to mine. His shoulders look so broad all of a sudden in this intimate space. I study the curve of his nose, the thickness of his lips, those moles on the side of his face. Then I close my eyes and take in the deepest breath I can gather.

"I didn't bring you on this trip so I could use your story for my game." His confession comes rushing out faster than my brain can keep up with it.

Eyes open again, I am staring up at him, calm as can be, his truth spoken in the air between us.

I'm a little shaken by his words.

"Yes, you did. Why else would you do it?" I ask.

He shrugs, those shoulders rising upward while he shoves his hands in his pockets. "My dad did a bunch of great things while he was alive. I haven't done anything. I think, in the moment, I figured that by helping you find out about your mom, it would be me doing a good thing for someone else. But if I told you that, you wouldn't have accepted it. I wanted to do a selfless thing, I guess."

"And?" I ask, my throat constricted. I want to be grateful. I want to be mad. I want to be so many things, but looking at his face, all I am is scared.

His mouth pulls up on one side. "It wasn't selfless at all. Because I got to be with you. I got to know you ... and that was unexpected."

I nod and clear my throat. "So, I'm out of the game, then? No unicorn?"

He laughs, and the sound cracks the tension in my chest. His fingers brush my hair away from my right shoulder and he sighs. "I'll try to fit it in."

"Good. I was really banking on having an action figure and stuff." I smile up at him when his thumb traces my cheek, and I close my eyes under his touch. One step forward and I'm close enough to grasp onto his belt loops, anchoring our bodies even closer. I rest my forehead against his chest for a second, letting his fingers move across my neck before I speak again.

"You know how I said I wasn't going to ask you for that next kiss?"

"Yeah," His voice rumbles through his sternum, and I look up with a smile.

"I didn't need to ask. I've already kissed you before. That girl with the pink hair at the bar … the one you told me about with the bad pick-up line about not being able to feel her lips? That was me. In a wig … obviously."

His whole body relaxes and he looks up at the sky, blowing out a huge breath. "Oh, thank God."

"What?" I'm laughing at his reaction.

He steps into me and wraps me in his arms, his face hovering above my own as we hold eye contact. "Now I don't have to feel bad about fantasizing about two separate girls. You're the same. This makes things so much easier."

I press a finger to his lips and ask quietly, "You fantasize about me?"

"You have no idea," he says against my digit.

Slowly, I draw my finger down his lips then trace his jaw upward to his ear. "I want that kiss now," I tell him. And before I can finish the sentence, his lips are on mine, his body pressed in close. When he moves to pull away, a hushed moan leaves my mouth, and he goes in for another kiss, lips parted and tongue seeking. It's euphoric, being in this place, in his arms. I have to step back and remind myself of where we are. Every part of my body tingles and pulses, aches and wants. *I feel wanted.*

He straightens his black t-shirt and angles away from me to adjust himself in his jeans. Turning around sheepishly, he grins and comes in like he's going in for another kiss, but I hold out a hand to stop him.

"I'm sorry. I have to talk to Cline here. Then we can go and do this some more. Is that okay?"

Elliot's tongue wets his upper lip, and his lashes lower as he breathes. "Yeah, yeah, of course. I'll go get him."

I swear, I blink and he's gone. The emotions dammed up inside of me are threatening to burst under the happiness I'm feeling, and I'm lightheaded under the onslaught of it. *Joy.* I am *wanted.* He thinks about me. Being around me isn't something that bothers him or that he finds to be a burden; it's something he seeks out.

I don't know what butterflies are supposed to feel like in your stomach, but I'm pretty sure this is as close as it gets for someone like me.

And then Cline's head appears in that entrance, and those butterflies start to drop dead, one by one.

"Are we doing one of these, too?" he asks, and

he looks genuinely perplexed.

"Yes. You're the main reason I wanted to do this at all, in all honesty. Which is exactly why we're here: honesty." It's all rushing out so fast. I'm not calm or collected like I had hoped to be. The headspace I had wanted to be in has been obliterated. "I need to tell you everything that happened back when we were fifteen, so you can understand the situation. And if you still want to hate me when I'm done, then that's fine, but you have to listen to me say this just once, okay?"

He's stone still, staring down at me like I might explode if he moves. "Okay."

I start to pace around the area between us so that I can concentrate. "You were my very best friend in the entire world. I trusted you more than I trusted anyone. You knew everything about me, and I never felt like you judged me for anything. Until that day in the cafeteria. Do you remember that day? The day Patrick and Miranda said I ran away?"

"You were acting spaced out and weird and then ran away from the lunch table and didn't come back for, like, a week." Cline is standing his ground, his eyes following me as I move.

"You called me out at lunch, asking me what was wrong with me."

"Shit, Audrey. I asked you if it was all my fault."

"It wasn't!" I stop and hold both hands up to make him be quiet. "This is the part I need you to understand. You asked me what was wrong with me, and Cline, I knew there was something going on with me for a while before that. I just thought I was keeping it a secret. But if *you* saw it, then I wasn't as good at faking it as I thought. I was sitting there feeling alone in the middle of a cafeteria full of three hundred students and my very best friend in the entire world.

"So I went home to ask my dad about it, and that's when I heard Miranda talking to him about having more kids. But he said, no, because *he can't have kids*. Not because of a vasectomy. Because he could *never* have kids. She's screaming at him that he's raising another man's kid already so why not do it again?" My feet stop moving, and I take a huge breath, turning to gage Cline's reaction. His mouth is slightly open and his eyes are wide.

"You know how Miranda treated me. You remember. Then I find out that not only did I kill my mother during childbirth, but the guy everyone thinks is my dad, isn't? On top of that, I'm … drowning. Just *drowning*. I don't have anyone to turn to, because the entire town thinks I'm this person … this baby who they helped save and raise, but it turns out I'm not even related to Patrick Byrd at all. My grandma hates me. Miranda hates me. And the only person who knows me has no clue who I really am, because *I have no clue who I really am.*"

"So you ran away," he states it and clenches his fist, wanting so badly for it to be true.

I shake my head. "I tried to disappear."

"What does that even mean?" His voice is bare-ly above a whisper and I can't bring myself to look at him when I continue.

"I'd been feeling that way for months. Maybe longer. I don't know. Like, maybe if I just disap-peared, everyone else's life would just be better. I would think of scenarios where I never existed in the first place. My mom would still be alive—all that. And it just became so clear that the problem was me. Miranda had been telling me ... but for the first time, I really understood that if I wasn't there, then things might be better for everyone. So after she went out with her friends and Patrick went to bed ... You know that detached garage where we parked the cars?"

"Don't, Audrey." He takes a step forward and I stand firm.

"You see it in the movies. It's like going to sleep, I guess. I just didn't count on Miranda com-ing home so soon and finding me. She was *so* pissed. Thought I was trying to get Patrick's attention. They took me to a hospital outside of town where no one would know and then made up the story about me running away. I got a shrink. I got these meds. I got a girl who calls me every Tuesday to check and make sure I'm still alive. I got fat. And I lost everything I ever knew ... including you. Because I couldn't face reality. And I didn't want you to think it was your fault." Finally, with sweaty hands and a heart that is beating way too hard in my tightened chest, I allow the feelings to rush in.

Tears begin to prick my nose, and my throat closes a bit as I stare into the face of the one person who meant more to me than anyone else in the entire world. "It wasn't your fault, and now that I've told you, I know you're going to look at me differently again. More than you did before. And that's okay, because what I was supposed to do here was ask you to forgive me for not telling you the truth sooner. I'm sorry I cut you off and didn't believe you'd still be my friend if you knew. Maybe you wouldn't have, but I never even gave you the chance one way or the other. So, I'm sorry. This isn't your fault …" I can't form words anymore because I'm crying so hard.

Telling the truth is supposed to set you free. It's supposed to give you a new beginning. For me, it simply feels like every last thing I thought about myself is true, and now that I've said it out loud, I've given it life. I've relived it and made it real instead of letting it stay on a movie reel inside my mind.

My knees begin to shake, and I reach out to support myself on the inside of that hollowed out tree, but I'm met with the strong arms of my former best friend as he pulls me to his chest for the first time in over six years. There's comfort there that I've sought after for so long that it knocks the wind out of me. I find the strength to wrap my arms around him, too, when he assures me, "It's not your fault, either, Byrdie. I'm so sorry for my part in it. I had no idea."

He makes a strangled sound, and I pull away to

look up at him through my tears. "Are you crying, too?" I ask, wiping the wetness from my face.

Cline's eyebrows are drawn together, and his face is sweaty as he shakes his head back and forth. "No. There's a bug crawling up my leg, and it's getting really close to my boxers. I don't want to ruin the moment, but another two inches and it's gonna be on my balls."

I push him away and crouch down, folding over as I laugh and cry at the same time, listening to Cline let out a scream like a little girl as he unbuckles his belt and turns his back on me to run out of the tree and drop his pants outside. I don't care that there are bugs on my feet and legs. I don't care that I'm alone laughing through my tears. I don't even care that I'm covered in sweat from telling him everything I've been holding inside for six years.

I did it.

I did the scariest thing in the entire world: I told my truth.

Elliot

There's something to be said about seeing your roommate run out of an old haunted-looking tree, dropping his pants and screaming like a woman while a beetle is heading straight for his nut sack. On my list of Hilarious Shit I've Seen, this ranks in the top five. Watching September run to his rescue, catch the beetle off of his manhood, and carry it away, though? Completely priceless.

Cline is sweating and pulling up his pants,

breathing hard and staring after her as I walk up next to him, unable to hide my laughter. "What? Were you not covered in bugs in there? Am I the only one because I'm taller than you? Is it my musk?"

"I don't think height has anything to do with it if they were coming from the ground, so, no. And I had a few ants, but they were worth it." I clap a hand on his shoulder while we watch the beetle being set free a hundred feet away.

"I'm gonna marry that girl. She took that beetle right off my balls like it was nothing. I have the weirdest boner right now." His face is twisted in confusion while he palms his zipper.

It is at that moment I realize Audrey is still inside the tree. "Is she still in there? Shit."

He waves his other hand at me. "We had a good talk. She's just getting herself together. She'll be out in a minute."

The fact that he says it was a good talk leads me to believe him, because had it gone sideways, his demeanor would have been very different standing outside. My gut instinct tells me to go after her anyway, so I approach the manmade door and poke my head in, hoping she's not covered in bugs and too terrified to move.

Audrey is crouched down, holding her knees and bouncing, her fingers brushing ants off of her shoes. She hears my footsteps and looks up, her eyes glistening in the limited moonlight. Without a word, she's on her feet and in my arms, hugging me harder than she's ever held me before. Her hands pull my face to hers, and she kisses me with so much force, I almost trip but find my footing just in time.

When she pulls away, I can see that she's been crying, but she's smiling while she sniffles.

"So it went okay? Did you get to talk to him about everything you wanted to?"

She nods and presses her cheek to my chest, squeezing me once more. "Yeah. I think we're going to be okay. I think everything's good again."

She's quiet on the way back to the house, staring out the window at the sky, but holding onto my hand as tight as she can. Her fingers don't tap, and they don't shake while in my grasp. I lift her fist and kiss her knuckles, watch her mouth pull up into a smile even though she doesn't turn to acknowledge me in the backseat of that truck.

Inside the Worley house, Cline pulls Audrey into the living room, and they speak quietly for a few minutes. I keep my distance, because it's not my business, but my friend has a big mouth, so I'll find out soon enough exactly what's being said anyway. I have patience. He holds Audrey's hands between the two of them, and after she nods a few times, he tugs and she falls into him for a hug where she almost disappears inside his embrace.

It's hard for me to imagine them as kids, but seeing them like this now, it's obvious how they could have been best friends all those years ago. They just fit together. When he lets her go, her eyes find me and she gives a smile, tilting her head in the direction of the room we'll be sharing. I follow her silent invitation, and we meet on the stairs so that she can lead and I have a fantastic view of her ass the entire way.

"I'm going to take a shower," she says and starts to pull out some clothes from her bag. I have a sense of deja vu from just a few hours before. "I feel disgusting after being out there. Don't you?" There's suggestion in her question and tone. "Plus … we shouldn't get these sheets all dirty. It would be really rude." Before I can respond, she's disappeared into the bathroom and closed the door.

I'm stuck in one of those moments where I don't know if I'm supposed to follow her into the shower, or if I'm supposed to wait for my turn. There's a chance that I could use the bathroom in the hallway, and we could just shower at the same time. Why the hell are there so many scenarios?

Can't girls just say what they mean? *Elliot, come get in the shower with me.* So easy. Damnit. Cryptic girl shit.

I'm going to go with the third option of showering at the same time so that I don't look too eager but also want to be clean, that way if she's ready to go to sleep, we can do that. Or if she's up for something else … I'm ready for that, too. My bag is pressed up against the nightstand where her phone is charging and I jostle it, causing her cell to fall to the floor. It buzzes as it becomes unplugged, and I reach over to grab it so I can plug it back in when I notice the green texts and notifications along the face.

25 missed phone calls and quite a few very angry-looking texts in all caps from her step-mother, Miranda. It's as if Audrey hasn't even touched her phone—hasn't opened it—since we left school. I don't remember hearing it ring once, and she hasn't made or taken any phone calls as far as I can remember. I've spoken with my mom at least twice.

Cline has talked with a few friends and had a call from his mom more than once. But Audrey hasn't used her phone for anything. I wonder if this is the first time she's even turned it on.

I mull it over in the shower, whether or not I should mention it to her. If that's an invasion of privacy or not. I have a legitimate excuse for seeing it, but she could read too much into things, as she is known to do, and what's ending up to be a good day, could instantly turn into a bad one. It's still in the back of my mind as I finish getting dressed for the night and crack the bedroom door open. As soon as I see her sitting on the bed in a pair of underwear and a tank top, I almost forget my own name.

She smiles, and I can see that she's nervous through her bravado as she turns and crawls up to the top of the bed to pull the covers down. Her butt is high in the air, and the tank rides up her sides, staying there when she straightens up and looks at me over her shoulder. "Are you ready for bed?"

My mouth has gone dry, and I'm bracing myself for this to be another night of just cuddling even though she's throwing crazy signals at me right now. It's better not to assume. "Yup," is all I can manage to say. I turn off the light and crawl under the covers next to her, lying on my back, my body on high alert due to her closeness.

Neither of us move for a few minutes, and then she turns into my side and lays an arm over my stomach. Her fingers inch down until they're under my shirt and she's tickling my side, leaving a trail of goosebumps behind with each pass. The simple touch is already having an effect on me, one she notices when her elbow grazes a little too low. Her breathing changes just the slightest bit, shallow and heavy by my ear. It only takes a turn of my head to find her right there, our lips touching in a light kiss.

Her tongue trails along my lower lip and slides inside my mouth, and I turn on my side, rolling her onto her back to kiss her deeper. There are a lot of things that I like to do, favorite pastimes I've grown fond of over the years, and kissing Audrey is quickly becoming top of the list. She grips the back of my head, fingers sliding through my still-damp hair while she bites gently on my tongue. I pull back to move lower, my mouth on her neck and tongue on her collar bone, hands gripping handfuls of her breasts through her tank top while she arches into me from below.

The bed doesn't make a sound when I kick the blanket off and trail even lower, pulling her shirt up and running my nose over her stomach and across her hip to leave a kiss above the elastic of her underwear. I'm just about to ask if I can take them off when her thumbs slide into the sides and she raises up and rolls them down for me. They're discarded across the room and I'm staring up at her from between her legs as she maintains eye contact from above, holding herself up on her elbows for support.

The first kiss makes her exhale, and I close my eyes, concentrating on her taste and her sounds, the way her body is reacting to what I'm doing. Her legs tense up and shake while her hands tug on my hair to push me away for a second before her hips rise to my mouth again. She's sensitive and so responsive to the things I'm doing to her that at some point, her sounds become muffled, and I look up to see that she has a pillow over her face to try and quiet herself from being heard.

I reach up and pull the pillow away, my face inches from her while I replace my mouth with my fingers and she clings to me just like she did in the tent the first time. Her moans are short and high pitched, and she's biting her lower lip to stop, but it's useless, because her hips are meeting each pump of my fingers, and her leg is beginning to shake.

"Elliot," she gasps, pushing down onto me and rolling her pelvis against my stomach. She kisses me, her lips dry and breath stilted before she speaks again. "I really like you."

"Oh, good. I like you, too," I whisper and slide my thumb upwards.

"Oh! Oh, God. Oh … Ummm. I …" Her eyes are squeezed shut and her body begins to rock a little again.

I try to keep my tone conversational. "Yes? Was there something you wanted?"

"Jesus, Elliot. Please tell me you have something, or else—"

"Or else I'll have to keep doing this?" I ask and circle my thumb quickly before sliding two fingers upward. "That would be a shame."

Her eyes are on mine and she's trembling as she grips my side. "You're going to make me say it."

"I told you you'd have to ask me for it."

"You said a kiss. Not this."

I lean in and kiss her quickly. "You got the kiss. Now what?"

"Fuck." Her whole body is tense, and she presses her lips together in protest, but I'm still two digits deep. She snakes her hand between us and wraps her fingers around my shaft. "I want you," she whispers.

Her face is buried in the pillow when she says

it, so I turn her so that we're facing one another when I respond. "I want you, too." I'm off the bed and have my wallet in hand less than thirty seconds later. Another thirty seconds after that and I'm covered, crawling back into bed with her, completely naked while she still has that tank top on. Lifting her arms, she allows me to take it off, and then she's as naked as I am, there in the darkness of September's guest bedroom.

She's beautiful, no matter what her brain may tell her. No matter what fault she may find in herself when she looks in the mirror. All I can see are curves and breasts and a beautiful face anxiously waiting for me. Sliding between her legs, I position myself and lean forward to kiss her once more. Her eyes are closed tightly, and I brace myself above her on my elbow, using my other hand to help guide my way inside her.

Audrey tenses for the smallest moment, and then her eyes open and she's staring at me while I sink into her slowly. She's holding her breath, and the second I stop, she exhales and leans up to wrap her arms around my shoulders and kiss me once more. I try to make it last, try to keep a steady pace, but the way she's so wholly wrapped around my body and the sounds she's making with each of my thrusts is driving me to the edge much faster than I am prepared for.

With a maneuver I've only seen in movies, I try to flip us over so that she's on top, but it doesn't work, and there's a second of confusion where we're a tangled mass of limbs and "sorry's" before we get situated again and I have her hovering above me. With her hands on my chest, she sinks down until I'm fully seated inside, and my fingers are gripping her thighs when she raises up for the first time. I don't notice it at first, but her own hands have gone to cover her stomach, and she has her eyes squeezed tightly shut.

That will not do.

I call to her, and when she looks down at me, I pull her close, bending her forward so that her breasts are brushing against my chest with each of her movements. Her hands cup my cheeks and here, with no view outside of her face, her soft moans become louder and her once timid movements become a frenzy, as if someone somewhere told her *this* is how it's supposed to be. If I could think of anything other than how good she feels right now, I would try to stop her, but my brain is focused on one thing. Within minutes, I'm gripping her hair and telling her that she's going to make me finish, and then I do, my entire body tensing up and toes curling in the process. She goes limp in my arms and rests her face in the crook of my neck, still straddling me, breathing hard like we've run a half marathon.

Finally, she lifts herself off of me and turns so that her hair is a curtain across my stomach. I can feel her hands around my now softening dick as she rolls the condom off and then scoots off the bed. "I'll take care of this," she says and then disappears into the bathroom. There's the sound of water running and then I hear a trash bag being crinkled. She opens the door again and walks over with a washcloth. It's warm and she kisses me while she cleans me up.

It's one of the most bizarre things I've ever experienced.

"I have to pee," I say and roll off the bed to go into the bathroom. The harsh light hurts my eyes and my reflection looks crazy. There are red marks all over my neck and chest, my hair is sticking straight up, and when I look down, I notice that the trash bag has been tied off on a knot. I finish up and walk back into the room to see that the bed has been stripped and Audrey is nowhere in sight. Quickly dressing, I open the bedroom door and peer down the hallway to see her talking to September in front of the washing machine. They're far enough away and so absorbed in their conversation that I'm sure they won't hear me coming, so I walk as quietly as I can toward the laundry room.

"What happened again?" September asks,

pulling the laundry soap from the top shelf.

Audrey blushes and looks down at the floor. "I'm sorry. It's really embarrassing. I can get you a new set."

"We have plenty of sets." September adds the soap and turns to look Audrey over as she leans against the washer, one leg crossed in front of the other, arms folded over her chest. "I don't care that you guys had sex. It was inevitable. Just … were you a virgin?" September presses her lips together and her eyebrows raise. "Did you just lose your virginity?"

"What? No. I must have started my period early or something. All the stress from the past couple weeks …" She points to the washing machine.

I turn immediately and go back to the bedroom, into the bathroom, and sit on the toilet waiting for her come back into the room. She does, and I can hear her moving around, putting new sheets on the mattress. Once the lights go back out, I turn the ones in the bathroom off and slip back into the bed like nothing happened.

Like I didn't hear anything.

Like after only a couple of weeks, I don't know when Audrey is lying.

She is up before I am, and by the time I make it downstairs, everyone is around the table eating breakfast. She has that smile on her face that I now know isn't real and hides all the bullshit she keeps inside, and I hate the fact that she's using it on me right now. Especially after last night.

"We were just talking about how you should stay another day. You don't have any plans, right? Nothing pressing. You can work on your game here." September motions toward an empty seat by Cline, and I take the invitation, sitting down and reaching for some orange juice.

"I'm fine with it if everyone else is," I say without looking up. It's apparent that the decision has already been made without my opinion.

There's conversation about what we could do for the rest of the day that goes back and forth between Cline and his girl, but Audrey and I are quiet. She's distant, barely touching her food, and I'm pretending not to watch her even though I am. I have no preference what we do. As far as I'm concerned, the point of our trip is over. We're just on summer break now.

Audrey pushes her plate away and crinkles her forehead. "You know what? I have a really bad headache and I'm feeling tired. I think I'm going to go lay down for a while if that's okay."

"Did you not sleep well?" Our hostess is leaning on the table, very concerned.

"Your bed is the most comfortable one I've slept on in a very long time. I've just had a pretty exhausting couple of weeks, and I think it's all catching up with me, that's all." That smile is in place again, but her fingers are tapping, and I want to reach over and yank on them to make it stop.

She excuses herself, and I'm left at the table with the others, wondering if I should go after her or not.

Audrey

In the quiet of the guest room, I realize that it's the first time I've been alone in almost two weeks. Besides using the bathroom or some minuscule moment here or there, sitting on this bed, I am finally alone with my thoughts and the ramifications of everything that has transpired since we left Brixton.

I can hardly wrap my mind around how far we've gone and circled back in that small of a time frame. Dr. Stark would be proud ... *will be proud*

... once I report to her what I've accomplished. Except for the part where I committed breaking and entering on my maternal grandmother's property, but maybe she'll let that slide since it opened so many doors.

I'm exhausted, my body fully spent after doing so much in such little time. I've been chasing happiness for so long, and now that I've experienced it, the reality of it feels like a burst beneath my skin. A flicker that ignites and burns out so quickly. I feel so much but nothing at all, or maybe the nothing isn't really *nothing,* it's just a diluted version of what other people must experience. An echo of an experience.

Anxiety rushes through my veins as memories from last night surface and I curl into a ball on the bed, closing my eyes as the images come. I fucked Elliot. Not in the Hollywood movie kind of way. It was more of an aggressive—I need to feel this— why can't I feel this—kind of way. It made me a liar, because I didn't tell him beforehand that he was my first. It made me a liar because I didn't tell September the truth. The entire thing is soaked in deceit, and for God's sake, I don't even know if he thinks it was any good anyway.

Rolling on my back, I grit my teeth and inhale, stretching out so that the knot in my stomach can get some room. What if *I'm* the worst ever? What if all he thought about the entire time was how Chelsea's body looked instead of mine? Or the weird sounds I made? Or how awkward it was that I took the condom off and cleaned up and stripped the bed?

My hands are sweating now, and I can sense the wave of panic rushing toward me like a tsunami. Not good enough. Not good enough. Not good enough.

This trip is over. I've done what I came to do. Elliot doesn't need me for his game. I found out nothing about my mom's mental history. I've said my peace with Cline. Now what? Do I even have anything I'm supposed to be doing now? The sink-ing realization that the answer is no hits me harder than I expect and I roll over, pressing my face to the pillow and pull my knees to my chest again.

I am so tired.

It's raining, a torrential downpour outside of the school, but Elliot is pulling me outside anyway.

"I don't have a coat," I call to him, but he doesn't care. He's always a step ahead, his hand yanking me forward, and I follow because it's Elliot. Why wouldn't I?

He's not wearing a coat, either, just a blue flannel, and he's taking us directly into the storm. All I can see are raindrops dropping from the sky, buckets of water falling just beyond the awning. I brace myself for the onslaught of wetness and ice cold spray, but nothing comes.

We're standing perfectly still on the grass of the quad, staring at one another, holding hands in the middle of the rain, but the drops are not descending. They're paused in mid-air, frozen in time, glistening like diamonds suspended from invisible ropes all around us.

Elliot smiles at me from behind a couple of the raindrops, and I reach up to move them, sending them floating off into the distance with the smallest touch of my fingers. His face is fully visible again as he reaches up and brushes a few more drops aside so that he can see me clearly as well.

"What the hell, Elliot?" Nothing is moving. There is no noise, no wind, nothing is making a sound except the two of us. The entire world around us is frozen.

"It's a glitch," he explains like it's the most obvious answer in the entire world. "A gorgeous, wonderful glitch in an otherwise perfect system. Everything is paused except for us. We can go anywhere. Do anything. Where should we start?" He's full of curiosity as his fingers reach out to touch another glistening drop.

Where should we start? My mind reels with the possibilities. "Can we go back in time, or just stay here?"

"Anything you want."

There are so many options. The day my dad met Miranda. Just one different choice and she wouldn't have been in our lives at all. Or the day I ran home. Maybe throwing a drink at Cline would have changed everything and none of this would have ever transpired.

My heartbeat quickens. Take me back to the day my mother became pregnant with me. I'll stop it from ever happening.

But looking into his eyes, I know my real answer. I know where I would go if I had the choice.

"Take me back to the day I first met you," *I whisper.* "Let's run away." *His hand extends and I take it, watching as he turns his back and begins to lead. My head and my heart are at war as the words form and present themselves in my subconscious.*

I could love him. This could be what love is.

But this love could be my undoing.

I awake with a start, covered in sweat, Elliot's arms wrapped around my middle. It's night and the house is quiet. Somehow, I have slept the entire day away, and my mouth is sticky, while my head is throbbing uncontrollably. Bleary eyed, I untangle myself from his grasp and fumble my way into the bathroom. The light is so bright it causes my head to pound even harder, and I groan in protest. I feel terrible, like I have the flu. My head is spinning and my thoughts are scattered, but I try to focus on one simple thing: a shower.

As quietly as I can, I creep back into the room and grab some things to change into so that I can clean up, and then maybe I can get something to eat or drink. I've missed an entire day's worth of medication, but the timing is off, so if I take anything now I'll be up forever, and I don't even know what kind of effect that will have because I've never missed a dose. Not even once.

I decide maybe Cara or Dr. Stark will have an answer, so I grab my phone to take with me in hopes that they'll answer a late night call. As I shut the bathroom door, I check the home screen of my phone and notice all of the missed phone calls and texts I've been avoiding since leaving school.

Miranda's texts stand out the most, so I begin to read.

Elliot

There is a noise that pulls me from my sleep. It's faint but out of place, so it brings me out of my dream gently and then with a jolt. The room is pitch black save for light filtering out from beneath the bathroom door. I reach over to check the time on my phone and it's just after 2 a.m. Audrey must have gotten up after sleeping all day and gone to take a bath. Maybe that's the noise I heard.

I get up and go to stand in front of the door to

listen for the sound of her in the tub, but there's nothing. No slosh of water, no drips, no movement of any kind. Tentatively, I knock and wait for an answer, but all I get in return is more silence. Thinking maybe I'm wrong and she's not in there, I try the door only to find that it's been locked.

"Audrey," I call and knock again, worry beginning to crawl up my spine and prickling the hairs on my arms. There's a chance that she woke up and accidentally locked the door when she left the room. Maybe she's downstairs with the others. They could be watching a movie or drinking. Maybe they're reminiscing about old times when she and Cline were inseparable.

These scenarios play out while I take the stairs two at a time and skid into the living room where Cline and September are asleep on the couch. Whatever movie they were watching finished a while ago, and the DVD is continually playing the menu music over and over, the sound of which is putting my nerves on edge. Audrey is nowhere to be seen.

"Hey," I yell just a little too loudly and watch them both jolt awake. "I can't find Audrey. The bathroom door in the guest bedroom is locked. The light is on, but it doesn't sound like anyone is in there. Did she come down here with you?"

"No. We watched the movie after you went up to bed and just fell asleep a bit ago. I didn't see or hear anything." September gets up and checks all the doors then returns with worry etched into her features. "Everything is locked. Are you sure she's not in the bathroom?"

"Do you have a key?" I ask, my hands sweating and stomach turning in knots.

She grabs one of the all-purpose keys from above the door frame, and we all head upstairs together. Cline is mumbling something to September, and I crane my neck to hear what he's saying.

"What?" I ask, turning toward him before we get to the guest bedroom door.

His face is pale, and his eyes are wide as he

looks beyond me into the darkness. "I was telling her about Audrey's confession at the tree. She said that the reason she stopped talking to me was because she'd tried to kill herself when she was fifteen. She's in therapy now, though. And she's been *so* happy this whole trip."

"You'd be surprised how easily people can fake it," September says matter-of-factly as she slips the key into the lock. When the door opens, her hand flies to her mouth, and she turns directly to Cline. "Call an ambulance. Elliot, I need you in here now."

The sight of Audrey splayed out on the bathroom floor surrounded by pill bottles, white foam pooling at the corner of her mouth, lips turning gray, is an image that will haunt me for the rest of my life.

"Lift her up," September instructs, and I gather this lifeless girl in my arms, pressing an open palm to her chest to feel a faint heartbeat beneath my hand. September raises the toilet lid, and without any pretense whatsoever, she opens Audrey's mouth and sticks two fingers down her throat.

There's nothing at first, and then suddenly Audrey's entire body convulses and she gags, retching into the bowl. Her heart slams repeatedly against my hand, and she claws at my grip on her, but I will not let her go. September will not stop trying to empty her stomach. We will not stop trying to save her from herself.

"How many, Audrey?" She's asking, and there's only a choking sound and moan in response before she gags again.

Cline is in the doorway, phone in hand, white as a ghost. "Five minutes. They're five minutes away."

"Pick up all of these and put them in a bag. They'll want to know what she took. Get her purse. And here …" She slides Audrey's phone my way. "We'll need to get in touch with her emergency contacts."

September takes over for me, and I let Audrey go, watching her lay her head in the other girl's lap.

Her eyes open just enough to focus on me as I press the home button on her phone. I bend down and use her thumb to grant access to her contacts and she whispers, "I found out about my dad. Miranda told me everything."

The paramedics arrive faster than I can fathom, and within minutes, she's on a stretcher and being rolled out into an ambulance. September jumps in with her, and I'm left holding Audrey's phone and standing in the driveway with a shaken Cline and a stomach full of bile that empties onto the grass as soon as the sirens turn on and the ambulance drives away.

I don't want to look, but I have to, so once I've composed myself, I begin to scroll through the texts between Audrey and Miranda. The ones I had seen earlier were Miranda telling her that she was irresponsible for being at the lake house and that it was no longer her property to use. The next came to say that she was ungrateful for the amount of money they had put forth for the care she was being provided. Not to mention the money for school. There was one about calling her dad. Then, when she wasn't getting a response at all, Miranda had said that she was tracking the phone and knew where Audrey was. If she didn't call home immediately there would be hell to pay.

Audrey responded that she'd been on a trip. Said she would call her dad in the morning.

Miranda demanded to know where she had been, and I'm not quite sure why she did it, why she felt like telling the truth, but Audrey's text was honest. She said that she had gone on the trip to find out more about her mom. And in doing so, she thought maybe she would find out about her dad.

This is when Miranda's rage hits the roof. It's hard for me to read the words. I can't bring myself to understand the level of pain it must have caused Audrey in that moment.

YOUR FATHER? YOU WANT TO KNOW ABOUT YOUR FATHER? WHY THE HELL

WOULD YOU WANT TO KNOW ABOUT THE MAN WHO RAPED YOUR MOTHER AND RUINED EVERYONE'S LIVES BY GETTING HER PREGNANT?

There's no response from Audrey after that. I check her call logs to see if she tried to contact her dad or her therapist or anyone, for that matter. Nothing. Why didn't she wake me up? How alone must she have felt after reading that?

The hardest part to grasp is whether she believed that Miranda had told her, in no simple terms, that everything she had hoped wasn't true, *was*. Her mental illness is hereditary. From a man who did something so vile it ruined three generations of lives with one horrible act.

Cline has the truck running, and I'm still looking through her phone as I climb into the passenger seat, buckling myself in while I try to find the number I'm searching for. He answers on the second ring. Patrick Byrd must not be used to getting phone calls at 3 a.m. from his daughter's phone.

He'll be even more surprised with the screen-shots of the conversation I'm sending him between his daughter and his wife.

"They pumped her stomach. I think we got to her just in time." September is holding a cup of coffee in one hand, and her forehead is resting in the other. Audrey is in ICU, and we're all in some sort of limbo because we are not next of kin, so there's no entry. "We won't get to see her. You know that, right?"

I shake my head. That can't be true. I don't think I can bear to leave this state without seeing her and making sure she's okay.

"It's true. Once they get her settled and leveled out, she'll be in here for a couple days. Then they'll put her on a seventy-two hour hold. We won't be allowed to see her." She says it quietly like we just need to accept it, come to terms with it early, so that none of us are surprised when it happens and we're dismissed.

We wait until the sun begins to rise, and just as my eyes drift close and my head nods forward, I hear a man asking for Audrey. He's demanding to see her. My attention is immediately on the tall, thin man with light colored hair and wire-rimmed glasses standing at the desk. Given the amount of time it's taken him to get here, Audrey's dad must have flown in from Tennessee.

He's handed some paperwork, and he speaks sharply to the nurse behind the kiosk before turning and slumping into a chair to fill out the insurance paperwork none of us had the information for. Cline is the first to stand up and go to sit by his side. The look of relief that crosses Patrick Byrd's face when he sees his neighbor causes my chest to hurt. When my friend points over to me, and the older man's gaze lands on my face, I am struck still until he nods his head and waves me over.

"Mr. Byrd, I'm Elliot Clark. It's nice to meet

you." I extend my hand and he takes it, squeezing once before letting go.

"I wish it were under different circumstances." He glances down at the paperwork in his lap. "You're the one who sent me the messages from Miranda?"

"Yes, sir. I would apologize, but—"

"Nothing to apologize about. If I had known it was going on, I would have put an end to it much sooner. As it is, she's packing her things and moving out of my house right now, with the instructions to be gone before I bring my daughter back home." He's furiously writing on the paperwork, focused so that he can get it over with as fast as he can. He pauses momentarily and looks over his shoulder at Cline. "How did she find out that she's not mine? I never told her."

"That's a good question. She just told me the answer the yesterday, actually. I'm not supposed to know about the last time this happened … with the car …" They are staring at one another in silent understanding. "That day she came home from school early to ask you about her mom because she'd been feeling depressed, I guess. But when she walked in, she heard Miranda talking to you about having kids, and you were arguing about how you could *never* have kids, and then Miranda said that Audrey wasn't your daughter anyway, so what did it even matter."

The silence lasts for much too long, making me feel uncomfortable, like I'm intruding on an intimate moment between the two of them that I shouldn't be a part of. Mr. Byrd's eyes are fixed across the room as he takes in what he's just been told and Cline is just staring at the side of his face, terrified.

"Six years of therapy, and we never got an answer for that day. Two weeks with the two of you, and she's an open book." He nods and presses the pen to paper again.

"She thinks she was a mistake," I tell him quietly.

He chuckles and draws a hand down his face, clearly exhausted. "She's a miracle is what she is. You know, Wendy always wanted a child, and I couldn't give her one. After she was attacked, I blamed myself. I should have been there. I should have protected her. And then she found out she was pregnant, and she just smiled and said, 'Look at the good that can come out of something so terrible.' Like this tragedy had been an answer to our prayers. When she slipped into the coma, I thought they'd both die, but Audrey wasn't going down without a fight. When she was born and Wendy died, there was no way I could let her go. I never expected things to be like this. Genetics are cruel in so many ways. But they're incredible in so many others."

"Like how?" Cline asks, leaning forward to rest his elbows his knees.

"She looks so much like her mother. The best parts of her. The only thing I have left to remember her by. I'll be damned if I let her take that away by her own hand over something we can fix, starting today." He slips the pen into the clipboard and stands. "It was nice to meet you, Elliot. Good to see you, Cline. If you'll excuse me, I have to go see my daughter."

As he's allowed entry to visit her, I know then and there that it will be a long time before I see Audrey again.

I want to write a letter to my father, telling him that I believe in God. I believe in heaven. And now I believe that hell exists in more than one place. It's not just the one we read about in the Bible, or the one under base camp in a foreign country. Hell can exist in your own mind.

I've seen it firsthand.

Audrey

What kind of man raises another man's child as his own?

I have asked myself this question more times than I can allow myself to count anymore. Each time, the reason behind it was self-serving or because of some twisted guilt he must have felt. But while Patrick Byrd sits at my bedside, reading *The Giving Tree*, his voice, a touch louder than the steady beeping of my heart rate monitor, I now know all of those thoughts to be lies.

A baby made from violence, born in despair but raised with hope, I am not the child I always imagined I had been. My biological father may have given me DNA, but my dad kept me alive all those years. Pushing him out and turning my back on him to distance myself from whatever I thought was going on only served to make me weaker, embittered, as the years wore on. I thought he didn't love me, but I was wrong. He loves me more than I could fathom loving myself right now.

Had I believed my own worth and spoken up earlier, Miranda wouldn't have been allowed to treat me the way she had. But my own self-hatred and the belief that I deserved it or that she was right, kept me from saying anything. These things inside my head are a constant battle, and the majority of the time I lose; though it's usually in the silence of my own mind, behind closed doors.

I know I keep people at a distance because I don't want them getting too close. Most of my relationships since high school have been superficial, just for a fun night or two, and then the insecurities creep in and I remember how hard it is to be friends with someone like me, and it would be better in the end to let them go before they have to take on my burden. It's easier to keep it that way so I don't get hurt. So I don't feel the pain of losing someone. There is no greater anxiety than wondering exactly why you're not good enough to be in someone's life. What you've done or said wrong. Exactly what happened—trying desperately to pinpoint the minute that you crossed the line and made someone turn against you. And there is no greater sadness than having your depression listen to your anxiety's thoughts about why you're not good enough and then agreeing with all of it, because deep down, you truly believe you're not worth it in the end.

My dad believes I'm worth it. He sits in this chair while they check my fluids and nurses come in and out to change their names on the whiteboard, hanging by the generic flower painting that's been glued to the wall.

He reads to me or just watches TV. But mostly, he talks. We finally discuss everything that I've ever wanted to know, and hearing him say that I'm not a mistake and that I was wanted, regardless of the circumstances, causes all of those memories in my mind to shift and take on a different hue.

He says he's sorry, and I say it, too, wondering which of us means it the most. There are no tears in his eyes when he tells me that Miranda won't be at the house when he takes me back home once they release me. He's already spoken with Dr. Stark, and we'll begin therapy together once I'm settled back in. My father and I have a lot of work to do.

"What about school?" I ask, my mind wandering to the two boys I've ridden across so many states with in such a short amount of time.

My dad's glasses slip down his nose while he closes the book and places it on the stand by the bed. "I'll go get your things from the apartment. We'll bring you home for the rest of the summer, and once you're feeling better, we'll get you back in classes. But let's take it step by step. We have a little time."

A young nurse appears in the doorway, opening the curtains and checking the clipboard before writing her name and the time on the whiteboard. ANGELA is scattered across the board before she begins speaking to the both of us about the next steps. The seventy-two hour hold and psychiatric evaluation. I know this part; though this time I'm frightened, because I've now come to realize how much my dad means to me and how alone I will be for the next three days while he waits for me in some hotel while he tries to get some work done. While he tries to make some plans for me after I'm released.

She has a soft smile and wide blue eyes, and her light brown hair is pulled back into a low ponytail. Her slender wrists look so dainty in comparison to mine as she works her cold fingers across my arms and hands. "How's your throat?" She asks, barely looking up.

"Sore. It hurts." The tube and what I was later told were September's fingers have left it hard to swallow without a constant reminder of that night's decision.

Angela nods and steps away from my bed to add more notes on my chart. "The doctor will be in shortly to talk about the transfer. You're doing well, Audrey." There's a knowing look in her eyes like she's seen my kind before, and I'm not a false alarm. When she clears the doorway, I can hear her speaking to another nurse right outside in the hall-way, and she says just loud enough for me to make out, "Had she taken the other ones, she wouldn't be here. It's a good thing she reached for the bottle she did. That's a ridiculous cocktail to have a girl on at her age. But what do I know? I'm not a doctor, right?"

Chills erupt all over my body in the silence that hangs after her words. Had I shoved a handful of another prescription down my throat, I wouldn't be here to know the truth about my mom. About my dad.

About my entire life.

It took two weeks to change my whole life. So it came as no surprise that it should take two weeks to even start to put it back together again. After the hospital stay in Mississippi, there was a flight home by my dad's side. Settling back into my old bedroom in the basement of my childhood home was bittersweet in so many ways. Each time I looked out the window into the backyard, I was reminded of a memory with Cline.

Each time I looked out the front window, I could see his house, and all I could remember was the night I stood on the lawn and asked Elliot to come to that party at the lake house.

We went back up there one weekend, Patrick and I. He claimed it was for a little rest and relaxation, but I'm smart enough to know that when your therapist adjusts your medication and says it may take a little while to get into your system—and she's worried, so you should be watched closely—a trip to the lake is the easiest way for a parent to keep you within fifty feet of them at all times.

We swam and fished, though I couldn't bear the thought of keeping anything I caught. Patrick would just smile and look wistful. "Your mom was the exact same way," he said while unhooking a fish and setting it free. The words didn't sting in the least. We were nothing but a work in progress, one day at a time.

My contact with Cline was minimal, but it was there. After all I'd done to try and set things right, I couldn't allow myself to let him go again. We mostly text, and they are brief, just check-ins to make sure everything is okay. He's the dose of reality that I need, and I am a little more grounded each time I get a chance to talk to him.

I talk to Elliot even less, because the guilt that eats its way through my insides every time I think of him is too overwhelming for me. I don't know how deeply he was affected by my actions, because we've never addressed it. There's no easy way to bring it up, either. It doesn't seem like something you'd text a person: *Hey, about that night you took my virginity... I didn't try to take my life because of it. You were a good first time.*

He may not even know that he was my first, though I wasn't very convincing in my lie to September, so she could have very well told him about the conversation regarding the sheets. Either way, less than twenty-four hours after sleeping together, he was helping to save my life. I've probably screwed him up for all of eternity. There are no gift baskets or Hallmark cards for that kind of thing.

Three weeks after my return home, my dad went up to Brixton with a truck to pack up my belongings. It was the first time he'd left me alone, but I had a sneaking suspicion he'd given instructions for poor Cline's mom to be on the lookout for anything weird happening in his absence. This was confirmed when I finally called my old childhood friend and asked outright if his mom was spying on me from across the street.

"Look, your dad told my mom that you were home alone for the first time since, you know … the thing." He's breathing heavily into the phone, and I can hear the strain in his voice.

"Do I want to know what you're doing right now? Quick: Does it involve a toilet, September, or both?" I ask, pressing my face to the glass window pane by my front door to stare across the street while his mom is peeking through her blinds.

Cline grunts and something lands with a thud on the other end of the line. "For your information, I'm helping your dad load up your room, because I'm a fine fucking southern gentleman, thank you very much. But this bookcase you have crammed into your closet is heavy as shit."

"Not if you take the books off first. It's from IKEA. It legitimately weighs two pounds."

"Oh, shut up," he huffs into the cell, and then I

can hear my books being pulled off and thrown onto the floor.

"Hey! Those are my favorites. Some of them are signed. Be careful with them."

"Oh my god. Elliot, come take the phone away from me before I lose it." There's a shuffle like the cell is being passed back and forth, some muttering, and then a final "fuck!" before Elliot's voice is on the other end of the line. It's the first time I've heard it since the night he held me in his arms and helped to save my life.

"Hey," he says, all out of breath and a little distant, awkward, unsure of what to say next.

"Hey back. You're helping my dad, too?" A quick glance out the window reveals that Mrs. Somers has gone back into hiding, so I head into the living room and stretch out on the couch, trying to imagine Elliot, Cline, and my father all working diligently to take my things down and pack them up to bring back here.

"Of course. Like I'd leave the state of your

possessions in the hands of The Hulk over here? He only had two breakfasts today, so he's starting to get hangry. I'm afraid he'll start throwing things in boxes just to get done faster."

I don't even realize that I'm smiling until I start to speak again. "I appreciate your dedication. If he's currently causing damage to my book collection, I'm going to have to go across the street and tell his mom about that time I caught him stealing our neighbor's Maxim subscription when we were seven."

Elliot laughs and reiterates the threat. "He's being very, very careful with your books now. It's an interesting collection, I've gotta tell you."

"Why is that?"

"I don't know. I guess it just has more Young Adult than I pegged you for. Romance. Stuff to make you cry. Books they make movies out of. And, from the looks of it, you have a predilection for book boys with one leg."

I close my eyes and laugh, conjuring up the

best image I can of Elliot's face before I answer. "Nah. Real life boys with two legs top that any day."

Elliot

May bleeds into June, and June fades into July. July's warmth wavers on the roads outside, causing heat to shimmer off the asphalt. Even though we are some of the very few who have decided to stay around the college town for the summer—who are not directly involved in summer classes—there are plenty of people for us to talk to or run into when we *do* decide to wander out of our apartment. I don't have a lot of time to do that as I prepare my presentation for Ten2One. I've busted my ass, spending almost every available moment I have on perfecting this game concept in hopes that it will land me the position to present the mock-up and get a chance to earn an internship with them.

If that happens, I could very well be on my way to making this game myself in just a matter of years.

Cline insists that I take some time out to watch the fireworks from our building on the Fourth of July, and I do, but my head is in a different place, thinking about Audrey four hours away, in the same state, wondering what she's doing at this exact same moment.

She'd laugh at thoughts like this. Me sitting here wondering what kind of fireworks she's looking at. Or with whom.

These thoughts creep their way in, though, and I imagine her at the lake house with someone. I envision them watching purple and yellow explosions in the sky, and I can see her face clearly, imagining the way the embers fall and reflect in her eyes. When I blink, the person that she's with is me.

It's exactly the way I want it.

Cline is sitting at our little bar, eating cereal, when I walk through the door, holding my portfolio in one hand and a wilting black tie in the other. He barely looks up before shoveling another spoonful of sugary rainbow-colored mess into his mouth.

"How'd it go?" He asks, milk dribbling down his chin.

"Killed it." I throw my portfolio onto the counter and slide onto the stool next to him, exhausted. I've never been under so much pressure in my entire life, but standing in front of that room full of guys—people who I want to one day call my colleagues, my equals—I was assertive and at ease. I was knowledgeable and confident like that first time I took a bite of Audrey's Popsicle.

I swear, if God *made* people to make video games, then He had that in mind when He was putting me together in my ma's womb.

"They want me to start the internship halfway through the semester. It's going to kill me, but I have to make it work."

"You will." Cline tips the bowl back, chugs the remainder of the milk and then lets out a heinous burp. "You're almost a genius. Like, right under genius. Just a few points away. You can make this work. Plus, it's your dream job. And let's face it, what else are you going to do?"

"Yeah, you're right." My mom had told me to focus on school this year, and if I got the internship, I wouldn't have to get a job, which was the plan for this semester. I hate to put her in this position, but something like this could legitimately get me a job immediately after graduation.

"We should celebrate. Sep's coming up this weekend. Let's go get drinks … get rowdy. School starts soon, man, and you've been locked up in your room like some sort of hermit for the last month." He's hovering by the refrigerator, his hand resting on the handle. We're both quiet for about a minute before he speaks again, this time a little quieter than before. "Do you think Audrey's going to come back to school like her dad said she was?"

I shrug. "I don't know. She talks to you more than she does to me. I don't even know if I should text her to tell her about today."

"You should. She'll want to know. Maybe you can slip in a question about when she'll be back. Ask if she needs help moving. That's smooth."

"Let's think about this logically. She already signed up for classes. She has to be coming back. It's just a matter of where she'll be staying ..." I'm staring at him, and I swear we both have the same look on our faces, because we're both hoping that she'll come back, but neither of us know for sure. Nothing with her is guaranteed.

An idea begins to take form in my mind, and I move to my bedroom to change clothes and grab a notepad and join Cline in the living room. Before he can turn the TV on, I snatch the remote and throw it across the room.

"A simple, 'I'm not in the mood' would have sufficed," he says with a look of shock.

I lean back on our less foul-smelling sofa and prop my feet up on our coffee table, sending some bottles rattling as they move backward. "Tell me some stories about Audrey when you guys were younger. Don't leave anything out."

As soon as he opens his mouth, I begin to write.

The semester is about to begin, and suddenly the campus is crawling with people again. It's unsettling how easily these students, new and old, are moving in and going about their business like nothing life changing happened over the summer. And I guess it hadn't. Not for them, at least.

They didn't meet Audrey and come to know her the way that I did. They didn't spend days and nights in cars and beaches, hotel rooms and houses with her. They didn't watch her spiral down to the rock bottom and get left behind after all was said and done. They probably went to Florida, got drunk, laid, and tan.

Last weekend, I traveled home to see my mom, and the first thing she asked about was Audrey. I told her everything, and she listened with wide eyes, and a hand over her heart. She held me afterward, as if she was afraid I was going to break or something. As if I had already experienced too much loss in my life, and what happened a couple months prior would only exacerbate that. From my perspective, it made me stronger. *I looked death in the face.* It only served to make me see things more clearly.

I told her the truth. "I lied to you about the game I'm making. The one I got the internship for is a war game based on those letters Dad wrote to you when he was deployed." My explanation was as detailed as I could make it without getting too far in and over her head. When I mentioned that the main character was based off of him, she brushed her curls away from her face and took a deep breath, extending her palm.

"Let me see."

I didn't hesitate. There's a part of me that knew she would ask, so I was prepared to show her. When I pulled the picture up, she exhaled and her eyes narrowed, straining as she stared hard at my laptop screen.

"Incredible," she said, shaking her head, amazed. "It looks just like him. He would have loved this."

"Yeah?" I closed the computer and set it down on the table, then wiped my sweaty palms on my jeans.

She punched me in the arm. "That's for lying to me." Then she leaned in and kissed my cheek. "That's for being an amazing kid." When she placed both hands on my cheeks and stared hard into my eyes I almost flinched. "Does this mean you're not making that game for Audrey? I'm telling you, it will make you a fortune, son."

I didn't give her a straight answer to that question. The subject of my newest project hasn't given her consent or seen the final result, so I am saving a public reveal until she gives the proper okay to do so.

Now I have to wait until she's ready to see it.

I'm thinking of her as Cline and I grab a booth at McNaught's on the Square. It's packed tight with bodies. Three weeks into the first semester, our fellow students are clamoring for any chance to get wasted already. I can't hear him while he's screaming at me from across the table, and he's terrible at forming words, so lip reading is nearly impossible. There's live music, and we're right next to the speakers as well as the bar, so I'm nearing deafness within five minutes of being in the building. It's uncomfortably hot, too, causing every piece of clothing I'm wearing to stick to my body. What was once a light blue shirt now has a dark blue ring around the collar, and I bet good money there's a nice line down my back, also.

Cline's wearing black, but it doesn't hide his problem either. I'm about to tell him we should leave when the girls show up and slide into the booth with us. They're smart, wearing sundresses, their hair up in a ponytail and bun respectively. September sits next to Cline and gives him a quick kiss on the cheek while Tee smiles next to me and reaches for a menu. Her eyes are bright blue, and her hair is a dirty blonde, the complete opposite of the girl sitting across from her.

I can't hear for shit, and Tee is saying something, pointing at the menu. I shrug and point at my ears, the universal sign of 'It's too loud in here' and she pushes up so that she can talk loudly enough for me to hear.

"I have to make a call. Will you order me one of these?" She points to the menu, and I note the type of beer she's chosen. I give her a thumbs' up and she smiles, making her eyes almost disappear and her freckles fold into the wrinkles around her nose as she pushes out of the seat and into the crowd again. Across from me, September and Cline are deep in conversation. Who am I kidding? They're trying to lick each other's faces off. I've become so used to it by now it's starting to disturb me.

There's a flash of teal just beyond their conjoined heads, and I crane my neck to follow it through the mass of bodies that have accumulated in the small space around us, but it's gone as soon as it appears. A strange knot forms in my gut, and I move away from the table, scanning above all the heads I can while I push my way to the exit. It's out on the sidewalk that I see her plain as day.

"Audrey!" I yell, and watch as she slows a bit before resuming her pace like she didn't hear me. I call her name again and break into a run to catch up with her.

Her cheeks are bright red when I make it to her side and she sighs, slowing down to turn and look at me with exasperation. "Damnit, Elliot. You know I don't run. It's one of my biggest weaknesses."

"Why didn't you stop? I was calling for you." I reach out to move her hair from her face and she takes a step back, brushing her cheek against her shoulder quickly.

"I saw you, but you looked busy, so I thought maybe I'd text you later."

"How long have you been back?" The awkwardness between us is unwarranted. It shouldn't be like this.

"Since just before school started. My dad sold the house. It was a deal with Miranda for the divorce. Whatever. Anyway, he moved closer to campus, and I got new place, so things have been super busy. Sorry I haven't called, but it looks like you've been busy, too?" Her head tilts in the direction of the bar, and just beyond the doors I can see Tee making her phone call, leaning against the wall outside, smoking a cigarette. It all clicks into place in that moment when I turn my attention back to Audrey and she focuses her eyes back on mine. Tucking her hair behind her ear she gives a smile. "She looks nice."

"She is nice."

"You *deserve* nice, Elliot."

I deserve *you*, is all I think, but the words don't come out. Instead I say, "You look happy. Are you happy?"

She squares her shoulders and nods, only once. "I have nothing to complain about. They adjusted my meds. Things are good with my dad. I'm going to therapy and working stuff out that I never took seriously before." She stops then and goes quiet, thoughtful, before she continues. "Thank you, by the way, for that night. For saving my life. Dr. Stark said I should tell all of you that, face to face." She smiles again. "I would have done it without her telling me to, though. Just so we're clear." Her fingers are tapping in rhythms of threes and fours against her thigh as she says this, making my muscles tense.

"I made something for you. You should come by the apartment soon and see it."

Audrey winces like she's unsure if it's a good idea or not, her attention going to the entrance at McNaught's again. "Maybe. Just text me, and we'll see if our schedules match up. I still have the same number." She turns to leave, but before she can step away, I reach out and take her wrist, pulling her to me so that we're face to face, just inches away.

I make sure she's looking me directly in the eye when I say these next words, because she needs to hear them, and she needs to hear them from me. I know what she learned about her dad and how she was conceived. I am fully aware of her guilt for the way she was born. I've seen firsthand how she wishes she could just stop existing. With her hands in mine between us, I bend a bit at the knees and lower my voice so that only she can hear, "Before you walk away, I need you to know … I want you to know that I'm glad you were born. I'm glad you're alive. And I'm so glad you're still here." Without waiting for her to respond, I lean in and give her a kiss on the cheek, then turn and let her go.

I walk away and leave her behind. I have given her an invitation to come to my apartment when she's ready so that I can show her what I've made for her. If she won't come to me, I'll find out where she is staying, and I'll drop it off at her place. One way or another, she'll get it.

For now, though, I have a dinner with September and her sister, Thursday.

Elliot

Three weeks have passed and there's been no contact at all with Audrey. I haven't seen her on campus, and she hasn't called or sent one text since I spoke to her outside the bar that day. Her communication with Cline is growing more strained and comes in smaller amounts as the weeks wear on and as far as I'm concerned, it's now or never.

I can't wait for her to come to me any longer.

"Did you ask her dad for the address?" I slip the small disc into its plastic holder and place it inside of a bubble wrap insulated envelope.

Cline nods and quickly taps out a message that vibrates on my phone seconds later. Her address appears as a destination on my GPS. On the table in our living room sits that ugly-ass fedora he used to wear along with a note: "I bought three more. Play this, or I start wearing them outside your building and telling everyone I'm your cousin."

"It's not exactly a threat, right?" I ask, taking it in my hands and turning it over to put everything inside.

"I'm not sure of the legality of anything you're about to do, Elliot Clark. But Godspeed, my good man." My roommate gives a sloppy salute, and I stop myself from correcting him because I know my dad is chastising him from his resting place anyway.

I slip out into the night and to my car, driving the five miles across town where Audrey's new apartment is. I know which one is hers, and once I reach the parking lot, I kill the headlights and pull into an empty space that faces her front door from several spaces back, under the cloak of some trees. It's after 11 p.m., and the lights in the living room are on. I can see two shadows walking back and forth behind the shades, their movements mildly erratic. It makes my skin prickle, and before I can stop myself, I am out of the car and rushing to the stoop to listen for signs of Audrey in distress.

My ear is pressed to the door to listen, and I can hear two female voices, rising and falling in an irregular cadence. One is definitely Audrey, and the other I am not familiar with. But they are both speaking, one after the other, repeating the same thing. Like they're practicing a play of some sort. But the only words I can make out are about vaginas and flooding.

The hiss and click of a lighter, then smell of a cigarette catches me off guard. I spin in the direction of the sound and smell to see a girl from one of my lecture classes leaning against the door to the left. She has short red hair and bangs that are only about an inch long on her forehead. It's the only reason I would ever remember seeing her in the first place. That hair.

She has one arm crossed under her boobs and holds the cigarette in the other hand, eyeing me curiously. "It's loud, right? Nicki is auditioning for *The Vagina Monologues,* and it's non-stop around here. If I hear the word *vagina* one more time ..."

The voice that I assume belongs to Nicki screams it again, and the red haired girl rolls her eyes then takes a deep drag on her cigarette before throwing it down and stomping it out with the toe of her shoe. "Want me to bang on the door and tell them to shut up?"

I stare at her for a moment and then hand her the hat along with the note and envelope inside. "Yeah, but can you wait until I'm gone? And make sure this gets to the roommate, Audrey. She'll know who it's from."

Red grins and clucks her tongue. "You're kind

of a creeper. But okay. I'll make sure she gets it."

I should feel embarrassed by this statement, but I can't find it in me to care. Instead, I race back across the parking lot and get into my car just as she begins to bang on the apartment door and Audrey's head peeks out. They exchange words and she's handed the fedora full of stuff. Hesitantly, she steps outside and opens the letter, a laugh making her whole body shake as she reads it. Holding the envelope in her hand, she looks it over and then glances out toward the parking lot, but since I'm parked a few rows back and under those trees, she can't see me in the dark.

When she goes back inside, I take a deep breath and start the car to drive back home. It's only a matter of waiting now.

Tell me about Audrey. Leave nothing out.

Cline's memories of Audrey are what shaped

the game I developed for her. Starring her. It's nothing spectacular as far as graphics go. After talking with him and finding out that the two of them used to play games on his dad's old Atari ("The only thing he left behind before he took off with that bitch, Kendra") I decided to keep it basic. They're the only kind of games she knows how to play, so it's a bit of a throwback to 8-bit. Much like Minecraft or a few other games that are going back to their roots, Audrey's game is simple.

When she puts it into her computer, it will load, and on her screen will appear the name *She Dims the Stars* with some music that Cline put together which sounds like some music box she used to have in her room when she was younger. I have no idea how he remembers this tune, but he says that it's one of those things that gets stuck in your head and never really leaves … just hangs out there and suddenly pops up out of nowhere.

Game Audrey is a princess born into a land where everyone loves her. Tragedy strikes upon her birth and her mother dies, but she is so adored that the town helps to raise her. She is a wild little thing with a chubby best friend who wreaks havoc everywhere they go. They spend most of their time down by the water's edge, playing in the woods and camping under the stars. It's there that young Audrey discovers that she has wings and is far different from everyone else around her, so she tries to keep the wings a secret.

A wicked step-mother enters the picture, and with her comes clouds of darkness over the land that Audrey once played around and where she found so much happiness. This woman finds out about the wings and steals them, leaving Audrey helpless and grounded. Desperate and confused. Her best friend has disappeared as well.

This is the beginning of her journey.

In Level 1, she'll be made to search for her way out of the town. Of course, I've provided her with exactly what she's asked for: a unicorn. Though, to be fair, it's an alicorn because it has wings to fly like a Pegasus, but it's a unicorn, too. Cline and I agreed that if a unicorn was going to shit cookies as a defense, then it should be from great heights so that the most damage could be caused—hence the addition of the wings.

I don't know how much time it will take her to find her alicorn, but once she does, she has to earn its trust, and only after they bond can she move on to the next level.

Level 2 is finding her best friend. As promised, I made Cline completely mute. He has no mouth, which I think she'll appreciate on *so* many levels. He, of course, has been banished to another land by the wicked step-mother and is being held prisoner by "that bitch, Kelsey" who Audrey has to defeat in order to save him. I have included the option for her to give him back his ability to speak or not, though I assume she'll opt to keep him silent. Wouldn't we all?

Once Kelsey is defeated, in whichever manner Audrey so chooses to take her down, and Cline is freed, he will lead her to a cave where his weapon is hidden: a fedora wearing dragon. Now, it's not my fault that this dragon exists. It's also not my fault that the dragon can talk instead of Cline. What *is* my fault is that the dragon mostly talks in innuendo and bad pick-up lines. So when they first meet, he definitely asks her, *"Do you like dragons?"*

She can choose to slay him or let Cline have something to ride. I, once again, assume she will let him keep his dragon, even if he's a major douche. The two of them, at this point, can continue on to the next level.

Level 3 involves the two of them working together to overcome the wicked step-mother. This part of the game is a little harder than the others because Audrey will be faced with a Miranda-like character who has an army of bat-shit crazy followers, doing her bidding. They follow her around and do her every command, attacking Audrey from all sides. The whole town seems to turn against her, but it's merely a mirage set up by Miranda, and if Audrey can figure that out, she can defeat her. In doing so, she can free the town, unlock her father from the spell he's been placed under, and she'll retrieve her wings.

Finally, Level 4 will appear on her screen, and Audrey will be alone in a dark room, standing in front of a mirror.

All games have one final battle, one final monster to defeat in order to win the entire game. The Big Boss is the biggest, toughest villain to beat and is the one that usually takes a few tries to overcome before you can call yourself a winner.

It's possible that Audrey will be confused when she sees herself step through the other side of the mirror and she is looking at a screen with two of the same character facing one another, identical in every single way.

I developed a scene for the doppelgänger to speak to Audrey, telling her that it doesn't matter that she's come this far. Nothing matters. It never will. She can't win this battle.

When I was coding it, Cline sat by my side, sweating and talking to September on FaceTime. "What if you trigger her and she relapses? What if you do something seriously wrong and cause her to go off the deep end?"

"September, do you think Audrey is strong enough to know reality from bullshit when she sees it?" I asked, looking up and into the pretty brunette's eyes through the screen.

She ran her fingers through her hair and exhaled slowly. "I hope so."

In any other game, this exchange would go on for a long time. The Big Boss would grow stronger with the main player's weakness. They would fly overhead and show their vulnerable spot on their belly or something to that extent. But this scene is silent with only the two of them staring at one another. After the fake Audrey stops speaking, a prompt pops up on the screen. Simple. One click.

Do you agree? Yes. No.

That's it. It's all she has to do. In order to slay

her monster, she simply has to say she doesn't believe the bad things in her own head. The stuff she hears with her own voice.

If she chooses no, which I hope she will, her wings grow, and she rises into the night sky, shining so brightly that every star around her grows dim. And with one swipe of her hand, the other Audrey is completely erased, obliterated into nothing but ash.

She's victorious.

I am nowhere in this game. There's a reason I did not place myself there to help her or to be a sidekick or the main character to save her. She doesn't need saving. She never did.

I gave her the hero she deserved: herself.

Audrey

It is three o'clock in the morning, and I can't stop shaking.

The music playing on my laptop is making my pulse race and memories of my childhood flood back long after I have beaten the game that Elliot made for me. This song was put into a music box for me by my dad when I was three. It was a song a friend had written for my mom years before I was born. I'd only recently retrieved the box from my room and asked Patrick about it.

He'd explained that Wendy was going through a rough time not being able to have children, and she'd had a best friend, Delilah, who played the guitar and wrote songs. She showed up one day and played it for my mom, telling her that no matter what, she was there for her through any and everything. He gave me the lyrics just last week, and I pinned them to my wall because they spoke so deeply to my soul. "It's okay to not be okay," she sang to my mother as she mourned the idea of never having a baby.

My eyes search out the paper with the lyrics on them, and I read them over once again, letting my heart stretch and pull while I picture Elliot putting all this effort into the gift he left at my doorstep. Without even knowing he'd done it, he'd woven a song of hope into his game.

Fear looks back
Doubt looks down

Hope looks up

So, darling, hold your head up now

It's okay to feel like the dawn'll never break

It's okay to not feel okay

Just remember me, friend, when you're down on

yourself

I'll be here with an outstretched hand

Don't worry, my friend, if you darken my door

'Cuz I'll be here to turn on the light

And I'll carry the weight of your dear, heavy heart

And dry the tears from your eyes

My lids are heavy, and I am drained from finishing the levels he created for me. The last one, choosing to not believe the terrible things being said about me, by the reflection of myself ... that was the toughest one of all. Psychologically, I wanted to agree, but in the moment, taking a step back and grounding myself in reality, listening to words of wisdom I'd gleaned from Dr. Stark, my father, Cline, and Elliot, I know better. It will be one minute at a time, and maybe I'll have to remove myself from the situation to get clarity, but I'll move forward every day. I swear I will.

Right now, I'm going to get my shoes on and go to an apartment where I have a sneaking suspicion the light will be on outside.

He opens the door on the second knock, hair standing up in multiple directions like he's been asleep, but he's fully clothed. The TV is on in the living room, and my first thought is that he's been waiting for me. He knew I would come.

Elliot steps aside as I walk into his apartment and I look around, comforted that everything is exactly the same as the last time I was there. Nothing drastic has occurred since the summer.

I turn to look at him, noting his glasses as he shoves them back into place and blinks a few times like he's trying to make sure I'm real and not some weird dream he's having.

"Count your fingers," I say. "If you have five, it's real life. If you have six, it's a dream. I promise, you have five right now."

He does as I say, and a smile appears on his face in place of the confused frown that was there before. "You got the game, then."

"Of course, I did. You left it with Tessa. There's no way it wouldn't make it to me. Good job on the fedora threat, by the way. I was thoroughly intrigued and scared. Put the game in immediately for fear that Cline would show up within the hour."

"He's asleep," Elliot says, leaning on the bar, his eyes still looking me over for signs of … something. Distress? I'm not quite sure.

Without asking, I move into the living room and plop down onto the couch, kick off my shoes, and turn sideways to look at him from across the room. "When did you have time to make it?"

"After I got the internship. With you gone, I had time on my hands." He's not nervous at all when he comes to sit by my legs. I scoot over to give him room, and the comfort of his closeness settles over me immediately.

I am levelheaded and focused when I speak again. "Do you think you love me, Elliot?"

His hand rests on my calf and he gazes down at his fingers while he thinks it over. "Do I think I love you? Or do I know I love you? I guess those are two very distinct questions, aren't they? Thinking you love someone means you're not really sure, and you want to test the waters. Knowing you do means you'd spend time with them, going through a bunch of states so they could find out about their mom. You'd stand in a dead tree covered in bugs and walk through cemeteries. Jump off a cliff. Risk being arrested for sleeping on the beach. You'd hold them until paramedics show up so they don't die." He looks at me then, his mouth set in a tight line and face deadly serious. "Do I think I love you? No. No, I don't think I do. It's pretty obvious to just about everybody that I know it."

I sit up and curl my legs beneath me, never looking away from him as I do. "My therapist asked me what it was like. My depression. The anxiety. She asked for an accurate description of the feelings inside of me when it's happening. There are so many ways to put it, but the best way I could describe it to her is that it's like being underwater. I'm constantly drowning, no matter how hard I kick, how hard I fight to get to the surface, I am always under the water, trying to breathe. I can see people standing at the edge with their hands reaching out for me to help me up, but I can't get to them. I'm like a raccoon with a shiny thing in my grasp. It's closed, and I can't get it to open no matter how hard I try to open my palm, *I can't*. Both fists are closed so tight that I can't get to the surface and take a hand for the help I need. I know that if I did, I would break the surface and breathe. I know there is air there."

He's watching my hands while I show him how tight my fists can squeeze. My knuckles are white, and the tendons are straining as I take a deep breath and exhale, unfurling them and leaning forward to touch his fingertips with my own.

"You're that for me, Elliot. You help me breathe, and it scares the shit out of me. You uncurl my fists. You stop the tapping by holding my hand. You squeeze my fingers when they're busy, *and you see me* … You see me do these things when other people would ignore it or think I was just weird. You have this way about you where you notice little things, and it makes you amazing, but it also scares me. If you see too much …"

"There's nothing else that I could possibly see that would make me run away." His hand is holding mine now and his grip is strong, a wordless promise.

"So, I guess I'm saying that I love you, too."

His smile gets so big it looks like he might be giving himself an internal high five or something.

"You should know I don't want kids," I blurt out, suddenly.

He leans back and makes a face. "Kinda just wanted to start with calling you my girlfriend first, if that's okay."

"Yeah." I laugh, and with it comes a couple of tears in my eyes that I reach up and wipe away quickly. "Okay. If you need labels and stuff, we can do that."

"I definitely need to have a label on this." He slides closer until we are face to face and our noses brush. "Otherwise, I have to keep using terrible pick-up lines like, 'Hey, girl. I just dropped a new single. It's me. I'm single.'" His eyebrows raise, and his mouth turns down as if to ask if I'm impressed.

"I *definitely* need you to call me your girlfriend, then. For the sake of all humanity." I don't wait for him to make the move. I do it on my own. Taking his face in my hands, I pull him in for a kiss, soft and lingering, running my fingers through his wayward hair. His glasses hit my face when I turn my head, and we both let out a laugh when he pulls back and takes them off.

"Did you like the game?" He asks, his hands roaming my legs and higher, making me squirm.

"Of course, I did. Your title needs some work, though."

Elliot leans back, fake-offended. "What?"

I shrug. "The acronym is SDtS which looks so much like STDs it's not even funny. You'll have a ton of people saying shit about it once it's released. Maybe just shorten it to *Dims the Stars*? I'm not a marketing professional."

"You want me to release it?" He asks, moving in again, crawling over my body on the couch, pinning me on both sides as he straddles my stomach and slips his fingers into mine.

"I'd be offended if you didn't. It's gonna make us millionaires."

"Billionaires!" Comes Cline's voice from behind his bedroom door. "Also, can you move this to the bedroom? I'm trying to get my beauty sleep."

"That much sleep is called a coma!" I yell to

him and watch as his door slowly opens and his head appears.

Elliot is completely still on top of me, and Cline walks toward us with tentative steps, his eyes wide and hands up in front of him. "Let's all remember that the coma joke was said by Audrey. I was not the one who instigated it. I had no hand in it …"

With a nudge, I shove Elliot off of me, and I'm sitting up next to him on the couch, looking them both over. "Is this how it's going to be? Eggshells? Because if it is, you need to stop that shit right now. I'm not a fragile fucking flower. I ride an alicorn." I nod my head for emphasis. "I slay fedora wearing dragons."

"No, you don't. He's your friend," Cline says, pointing a finger at me.

"I'm the hero in this game, boys. Don't you forget it." I stand and walk over to Cline, standing on my tiptoes to reach up and give him a hug. "I love you, you idiot," I whisper when he hugs me back.

"I have a girlfriend," he says back right before I poke him in the neck and make him fold in two, giggling like a doughboy.

Pushing him back, I extend my hand to Elliot, and he takes it, following behind me to his bedroom. "So does Elliot," I say as I close the door.

We're alone in his room, his piles of clothes still scattered about and wires still coming from every possible place imaginable. He sits on the bed and watches me while I settle into the desk chair and swivel side to side.

"Are you tired?" I ask.

He shakes his head no, and I turn some more, tilting my head to look up at the ceiling.

"Me either. What a conundrum."

"I can think of a few things we could do," he says, and I roll my head forward to look at him with an eyebrow raised.

"Does one of them include using your superpower?"

He makes a "come hither" motion with two fingers, and I nod.

"Yep. That's the one."

"Since we're on the subject…" His gaze lowers to the bedspread and he licks his lips before he speaks again, quieter this time. "That night. Was that your first time?"

"Would you be super shocked if I said that it was? I told you before that I'm not comfortable with my body."

"Why didn't you say anything?" The look on his face is almost adorable, but my cheeks are on fire and my hands are sweating so it's a little hard to appreciate.

I shrug. "You're awkward and I have panic attacks. Did you really think that would go over well?"

He nods a couple times and blinks rapidly. "Fair enough."

"The truth is that you're the first person I felt safe with. And if you're wondering whether or not it had anything to with what happened afterward…"

"I saw the texts. I know it wasn't that."

"So sure of yourself," I joke, swiveling in the chair once more.

"I mean if you're not sure whether it was good or not, we could always try it again. You know. For science." He's grinning and that pull in my chest becomes so tight I can hardly breathe, but it's in the very best way.

"I could never deny science." I stand, cross to the bed, and crawl onto the mattress with him, lying on my side so that he mirrors my position. Our hands find each other and fingers link between us as we stare at one another in his one-lamp-lit bedroom. He's looking at me with such adoration, but there's another layer behind it—worry—that he's trying to bury for this moment between us. "I'm okay. I can't promise you that every single day is going to be perfect, but I what I *can* promise is that I'm trying my very hardest. It'll be amazing and sometimes it'll be terrible, but I'm in here fighting to stay afloat. For the first time in years, I have people I trust to talk to about it. Besides a doctor, I mean. You see me, and because of that, I don't want to disappear anymore."

He touches his nose to mine and brushes his lips softly over my chin. "And if you ever get to that place again?"

I lean back and hold up our hands between us, my palm open to his, fist unfurled. "I have a hand to reach for."

Epilogue

Elliot

I can't find Audrey in this swarm of people, and it's beginning to make me nervous.

"Elliot! Ellioooottttttt!" Cline is waving frantically at me from one of the vendor booths, his beer sloshing over the side of the cup he's holding in his hand. I follow where he's pointing and can't help but laugh at what he's freaking out about. A group of girls are waiting for the next act to take the stage, and they're all wearing a *Dims* t-shirt. They've cut them up so that they're basically shredded tank

341

tops, but if they want to trash a thirty dollar t-shirt, that's not my business.

Seeing a group of girls wearing our shirts with rainbow poop cookies on them at a four-day music festival in Memphis is a little surreal, though. Even after all these months.

A pink head of hair stops in front of me, and Audrey's eyes appear beneath the neatly trimmed bangs. She's holding VIP passes in one hand and cold water bottles in the other. "Did you see them? The girls in the shirts?"

"Of course, I did. Cline was freaking out and not being the least bit cool about it," I tell her as I take a VIP pass and a water from her.

September and Thursday arrive just seconds later, both wearing wigs as well, one bright blue and the other electric green. It was an act of solidarity when Audrey realized she wasn't going to be able to go to the festival without being recognized as the face of the wildly popular game/app *Dims the Stars*.

When a college kid makes that kind of money,

in that small of an amount of time, press gets wind of it, and then there are news outlets involved and magazines get called. I wasn't going to lie and say that I'd created it on my own. Audrey and Cline were stakeholders as far as I was concerned.

I paid off mom's mortgage. Put some money away for a rainy day. I still took the internship at Ten2One, but essentially they offered me a regular position, and I couldn't handle the load with school work, so they're holding it for me until after I graduate. If I still want it.

Who knows, though? I might just be able to start my own company after this.

It took an adjustment period for Audrey to accept that people related to her through the game. When she did an interview and shared her battle with depression and anxiety, the outpouring of support and people sharing their stories with her was overwhelming to the point that she actually had to go offline for about a week.

"I can't be someone's role model," she said.

Pale and shaking, she pushed the laptop away and shook her head over and over. "I didn't sign up for this."

"And if you save one life? Just one because you were honest enough to tell other people that they're not alone, and someone out there understands even just a glimpse of what they're going through … wouldn't that be worth it?" That was September, who we had to call, because it was one of those low moments that Audrey had said would happen but we were still unprepared for.

I think it took two days for her to let it sink in that what she'd been through could end up helping someone else. We had a discussion. I set up a website, and she wrote a blog. Then she added an anonymous question button for anyone who wanted to ask her anything. Some stuff was easy, and she answered it with grace. Others were harder, and it took some hand holding to get her through it.

The entire experience helped her find herself and her purpose, though. She works closely with certain organizations, like Project Semicolon, to spread hope where people may not feel there's any to be had. She even has a little semicolon tattoo between her thumb and forefinger. She says it's a reminder, a promise. Every time we hold hands and our skin touches in that exact place, Audrey knows that she has more life to live. She has more of her story to tell.

"Thursday, where is Micah?" Audrey asks, and the girl in the green wig points toward where Cline is standing, next to the tall redheaded guy we've recently come to know as her boyfriend. "Oh, no. He has that look on his face, Sep. He's going to do something stupid. You'd better intervene."

The sisters take her warning and run off to stop whatever ridiculousness *our* best friend is about to pull, and I take Audrey into my arms, pulling her close as the crowds start to shift forward for the next band.

One year is all it took to change my life completely.

One moment to shift it on a different course.

One second of a stranger's kiss—a rock on a window—a call from out of the blue.

All of it started with one girl and a question.

Audrey is leaning back against my chest while the music begins to grow louder and the crowd starts to get more amped up. Without her having to ask, I walk us backward until we're away from the center of the madness, holding her in place against my body. She's safe here with me. Always has been and always will be.

She turns and looks up at me from behind neon yellow glasses, then pulls them down off her face and tilts her head to the side to give me a wistful smile. "What?"

I brush a strand of pink away from her forehead and lean in to kiss her mouth, cradling the back of her head so that I can look her in the eyes when I pull back. "Run away with me," I say and press another light kiss to her parted lips.

She smiles, her eyes so full of life and mischief,

as she places the sunglasses on top of her head. "Name the time and place, Elliot Clark. I'm all yours."

These words I know are true.

Somehow, I know they always will be.

I plan to watch Byrdie fly for the rest of my entire life.

Author's Note

Hello, sweet reader! Thank you for taking a chance on me. On this book. On Audrey, Elliot, and Cline.

It should be noted that Bertram Falls, Tennessee does not exist. Neither does the fictional Brixton College (just my homage to the late Mr. Bowie). The Confession Tree is not a real thing, however the cemetery and bridge that are described leading to it are very much a place that can be visited – but I would advise against it.

Audrey, though… Audrey does exist in one way or another. She's someone you know, or knew, or she's possibly a little bit of you.

I wrote this book for a very specific reason and that was to show another side of anxiety and depression that doesn't get a spotlight very much: the hidden kind. The kind that's folded away behind a nod and a smile, a joke or a laugh, an entire night out with friends that leaves that person exhausted for days afterward having to recharge because being 'on' all the time takes so much out of them.

Depression is a hard topic to discuss. It's hard to understand. And even deeper than that? If you have experienced it, your depression may not be the same as someone else's. It may not be the same as mine. You could ask a million people what their experience is like and you might hear that 90% of what you've experienced is the same, but the other 10%?

Mine and yours alone

Depression is an ugly, ugly thing. It starts small and grows until it's like those vines around trees that envelope the entire plant until it's suffocated and the intruder is satisfied and full because it's taken the host's life source. Even when you are doing your very best to fight it, depression and anxiety kinda hold your hand and pop in every once in a while like that annoying neighbor you try to deter from visiting by turning off your porch light.

They know you're home, though. They persist. It persists.

Even on medication that is supposed to help with this mess, the depression creeps in. It hovers and seeps and tries to vine its way in. But I fight. *You fight.* They fight. Every day we face the battle to hold the hand of the one who keeps us down or look up and hope that we can say that today was a good day.

So trust me when I say that I know about 90% of what you're going through. And because of that you are NOT alone. Some of us are silent in our suffering and others will look you straight in the eye and say that we're in pain. I know, beyond a shadow of a doubt that no matter which side of the fence you're on you need to hear something that will make you see the light and the only thing I can offer is this:

I am glad you're alive. I'm glad you were born. I'm glad you're still here.

You keep up the good fight, okay?

You are the hero in this game. Don't you ever forget

it.

Xoxox,

Amber L. Johnson

Acknowledgments

First and foremost I have to thank my husband and my son for giving me a month and a half of Sundays to complete this book. AJ and EJ, those precious few hours you gave me in a quiet house made all of this possible. A, thank you for always being my inspiration, you video game creating genius. E, I'm sorry I ate all the Halloween candy in the process of getting this finished. Mostly. I'm mostly sorry I ate it all. There are a few pieces left in the freezer.

I tried to find a way to thank Dylan O'Brien for his face, Miles Teller for his mannerisms, and coffee for getting me through all those early mornings without sounding like a weirdo, but that's not going to happen. It is what it is.

Stephanie DeBear, my writing partner, critique partner, and the reason half of the weirdest pieces of the dialogue in this book exist thanks to our real life texts - Thank you. We both know I'm crazy, but you signed on for life, and you can't back out now. It's in the contract. Your genuine enthusiasm to see me be successful makes me want to cry, but that would ruin my make up so let's stop that right now. Our collective brains are now responsible for rainbow poop shitting unicorns, penis throwing octopi, and scrotum beetles. Our parents are so proud.

Lori Wilt, thank you for loving Audrey and Elliot for the last three years, back when they were part of a YA book called 'Falling for the Girl Next Door.' I know they don't resemble the original characters much, but you've stuck by my side as I trudged my way through this process and chipped away at them until they became who I wanted them to be. You're the driving force in all of my soundtracks.

Amber Sachs, Lynsey Johnson, Dani Hart, Angela

Williams, Nicki Firman, and Mandy Arthur: reading your feedback and responses as you experienced the book was such a joy for me. You helped me in more ways than you will ever know, the biggest of which being to push me to actually publish this book and to keep writing, no matter how hard it was at the time. You kept me going. I owe you big time. And I adore you endlessly.

Thank you to my editors: April Brumley, thank you for swooping in so fast and for turning things around just as quickly. I swear I will never call a man's bathing suit swim trunks again. And Catherine Jones, you are incredible. Thank you for making this manuscript look so pretty before it went to print. Karen D. I appreciate you taking time to work on the first half of the book. I'll never look at run-on sentences the same!

Amber Maxwell, thank you for the beautiful gift of the Dims cover. It far exceeded my expectations and continues to take my breath away. You are a true artist and I'm blessed to know you.

Lindsey Gray, thank you for making my book look so gorgeous. Your formatting skills are always impeccable and I know I can always count on your professionalism whenever we work together.

Nurse Angela VanBuren, thank you for making sure our girl got the right help she needed in the hospital. You always give me the best medical advice and if I ever ended up in the hospital in your state, I would demand to be seen by you. I heart your face.

Jocelyn, my September in July...thank you for allowing me to use your likeness and your face. We've been friends for over 10 years. Legally, we're sisters now.

Laura, my Delilah, thank you for your gift of song and for allowing me to share it with the world. We're beyond common law friendship too, now. I'm your other sister. Tell Kelita sorry-not-sorry.

Huge thanks to The A Team, my street team on Facebook who helps spread the word about my new releases. I am honored you'd spend your time with me.

You are the actual best. I'll make you t-shirts to prove it.

To Mariana's Trench for being the never ending loop that I listened to while writing this book: Thanks for the harmonies, the imagery, and the lyrics that kept me going, even when writer's block settled in.

Lastly, to you the reader, for taking a chance on this book. Personal stories are super scary to write. They are terrifying to share. Having someone believe in them makes it all worthwhile.

Purchase a copy of It's Okay by Laura Engelbrecht

(an original song written for She Dims the Stars)

Song List

1. Cecilia & the Satellite - Andrew McMahon & The Wilderness

2. First - Cold War Kids

3. I Am -AWOLNATION

4. Underdog - Imagine Dragons

5. Four of July - Fall Out Boy

6. Ever After - Mariana's Trench

7. Water Under the Bridge - Adele

8. A Little Too Much - Shawn Mendes

9. Roses - The Chainsmokers

10. Molecules - Atlas Genius

11. Believe - Mumford and Sons

12. Cocoon - Catfish & the Battlement

13. Chasing Stars - Fleure

14. Pieces - Hushed

15.This Love - Taylor Swift

16.Pretty Little Girl - Blink 182

17.What If - Safety Suit

18.This is Gospel (Acoustic) - Panic! At the Disco

19. It's Okay - Laura Engelbrecht

http://www.projectsemicolon.org

MISSION STATEMENT

PROJECT SEMICOLON IS A GLOBAL NON-
PROFIT MOVEMENT DEDICATED TO PRE-
SENTING HOPE AND LOVE FOR THOSE WHO
ARE STRUGGLING WITH MENTAL ILLNESS,
SUICIDE, ADDICTION AND SELF-INJURY.
PROJECT SEMICOLON EXISTS TO ENCOUR-
AGE, LOVE AND INSPIRE.

STAY STRONG; LOVE ENDLESSLY; CHANGE
LIVES

National Hopeline Network :: 1.800.SUICIDE (784-2433)

National Suicide Prevention Lifeline :: 1.800.273.TALK (273-8255)

For hearing and speech impaired with TTY equipment :: 1.800.799.4TTY (779-4889)

Español :: 1.888.628.9454

About the Author

Amber lives in Texas with her amazingly talented husband and incredibly gifted son. Most known for her novella Puddle Jumping (a 2014 Goodreads Choice Award nominee for Best YA) she is constantly trying her hand at new genres and ideas to force herself to think outside the box.

She is inspired by music, her family, a close group of friends, and real life. Mostly in that order.